9-00
5-02
9-11
3-17

What do you call a kitten with a Colt .45?

Worthy turned his head toward Jessica and she suddenly pushed him to one side. A man had appeared in front of them with a pistol. The gunman ignored her, aiming point-blank at Worthy. There was only a second. Jessica tilted her handbag up and fired through the bottom of it. The gunman's shot tore into the ground at Worthy's feet as the man slumped, dropping his pistol.

Worthy swore in surprise, staring at Jessica. She knelt by the would-be assassin and felt for a pulse. There was none. She shook her head, gathered up his pistol, and motioned to Worthy. "Go that way!"

He did as she told him. This beautiful young woman was a *tigress*!

WESLEY ELLIS

LONE STAR

AND THE
BARBARY KILLERS

JOVE BOOKS, NEW YORK

LONE STAR AND THE BARBARY KILLERS

A Jove book/published by arrangement with
the author

PRINTING HISTORY
Jove edition/April 1989

ISBN: 0-515-09986-4

PRINTED IN THE UNITED STATES OF AMERICA

10 9 8 7 6 5 4 3 2 1

Chapter 1

It was a night of stagnant fog that blurred the lamps and short-ened the distances. It was cold; clammy hands touched his face and Carlos Ortega, the Bancroft carriage driver, hunched his shoulders as he eavesdropped on his mistress and master's arguments in the coach behind him.

He had driven this route a hundred times and paid scant attention to the steep hill they climbed. The Bancroft lead carriage horse, Mathilda, knew her way around the Nob Hill streets in the thickest of fogs. Carlos let her go as she pleased.

His attention riveted on the conversation so close, Carlos let the reins droop.

His mistress's voice was sharp, almost strident: "What business could you possibly have with that awful Josiah Kel-ton?"

"Please, Penny, leave our financial affairs to me! I've done right by you so far, haven't I?"

Ortega turned slightly to see his employer, W.R. Bancroft, Sr., tuck a wisp of his wife's graying hair under her diamond tiara and pat her cheek affectionately. W.R.'s voice had been harsh, but Ortega had been with the family too many years to be fooled by a tone. He was well aware that his employers were as much in love now as they had been many years ago when he first came to work for them. Was it two decades!?

A vagrant breeze swirled the mist into eddying spirals,

1

coppery in the light of the coach lamps. Ortega sighed and pulled the coat more tightly about his shoulders. Mathilda and the companion horse nodded as they plodded up the hill, their hoofbeats on the hard-packed road were the only sounds in the night. He gazed fondly at the lead animal. Whenever the Bancrofts planned to be out after dark, Ortega always made sure that Mathilda was one of the team. In his opinion, she was as sure-footed as any animal alive.

He thought about the warming fire, not far off now, where he would shuck his coat and sip something hot, perhaps with a bit of gin in it. He smiled in the night as the fog frothed and curdled about him.

This was the only carriage out at this late hour. Pedestrians had long since fled the evening's penetrating chill, locking doors and shutters behind them.

He leaned back, listening to the murmurs of the voices in the coach behind his shoulder; they were speaking more softly now. Ortega knew that Mrs. Penelope was searching for the truth in her husband's light blue eyes, but he knew too that she would see only the troubled lines that in the last few months had become so familiar.

Her voice was stronger: "Darling, please share your problem with me! Don't shut me out after twenty-five years! We started out together with nothing, and I stood by you then—"

"Of course, you did . . ."

"Why won't you let me stand by you now?"

"But dear—"

"I know there's something very wrong, and that Kelton person is at the bottom of it."

"But dear, there's nothing—"

"Oh, stop it, W.R.! Six months ago you would have laughed at anyone suggesting that you even consider accepting an invitation to a dinner party at Kelton's. But tonight you allowed him to humiliate you and degrade us both!"

Carlos Ortega shifted uncomfortably, hearing the tears in his mistress's pleas as she attempted to pull the truth from her husband. He himself thought she was right. There had been a change in Mr. Bancroft.

Carlos glanced to his right. Were there shadows there, among the deeper shadows? He felt the reassuring bulk of the pistol at his hip under his coat.

Mrs. Bancroft was speaking again, but in a low voice he could not hear. Carlos blinked and looked around him. What could possibly happen on this familiar stretch of road so close to home?

Of course, there was always the possibility. He pulled the heavy pistol from under his coat and rested it on his thigh. Mr. Bancroft had shown him how to use the gun, and it made him feel much better. The cold steel was his friend.

Ortega frowned, glancing from side to side, his thumb on the hammer of the pistol. He must remember to pull it back before it would fire.

He realized then that the carriage was approaching Dead Man's Drop. Someone long ago had named it, and no one quite knew why. Presumably a man had fallen at that point. But it was a curve respected by everyone on San Francisco's fashionable Nob Hill.

"Steady girl," he said breathily as the team stumbled and the companion horse whinnied in alarm. Even Mathilda shied. Something was spooking her. Usually the most placid of all the horses in the Bancroft stables, she pulled against the reins, tugging and trying to turn. Ortega stood in the box and slapped the reins. "Steady! Steady!"

What was the matter with her? He swore under his breath.

Then Mathilda reared up, and in the next moment, she bolted!

"*Dios mio!*" Ortega shouted. "Stop. Damn you!" His foot wet with mist, slipped off the brake, and the lurching coach threw him off balance as the reins went flying. He heard his passengers yell in surprise. Mrs. Bancroft screamed in fright, and Mr. Bancroft roared. Ortega's thumb pulled back the hammer of the pistol—he did not know he had done it—and his finger tightened on the trigger. And the gun suddenly fired.

In an instant, the horses dashed forward, swerved suddenly away from something to their right, and ran straight for the cliff of Dead Man's Drop!

The heavy wooden barrier splintered as the team burst through. The shock spilled Ortega from the box. He had a moment's sensation of flying through the air; then he landed hard, very hard, the breath knocked out of him. He lay in a heap, aware that Mathilda was whinnying in terror. Someone screamed all the way down the drop. Ortega heard the carriage crash and shatter as he struggled to breathe, trying to sit up.

His head felt full of cotton—he could not think. But he could still hear Mrs. Bancroft screaming. She seemed miles away from him. . . .

But something else entered his woozy consciousness, another sound. From somewhere off to his right, Ortega was dimly aware of several spectral figures, more vapor than being, one of whom seemed to giggle. Then a twig snapped as the figures moved, and Ortega realized they must be real.

His consciousness faded and a suffocating blackness closed about him, blessedly shutting out the horrid sounds of the screaming at the base of the cliff.

It was nearly dawn when Carlos Ortega woke, the pain seeming to jolt him. He felt himself—nothing was broken—and he could stand, sucking in his breath. The screaming had stopped. When he looked down he could see the outline of a smashed carriage, but nothing moved there. Both team horses were obviously dead, and he knew, with a deep sigh, that his employers were, too. How could either of them have escaped?

He looked around him. No one had stopped to investigate, probably because he had been hidden by weeds as he lay in a heap. And apparently no one had heard the shot or the crash. The fog must have blanketed both sounds and helped to hide him from passing eyes.

It was still foggy and clammy cold. He sat on the edge of the cliff, holding on to the splintered stump of the barrier. Did he hear sobs from down below? It was hard to tell. He took several deep breaths. He must make his way down the cliff and see.

He had no rope, and he was no longer a young man. He waited till there was more light, then with a prayer to his patron saint, he started inching his way down, holding on to every bush and fold of earth, sliding, swearing when it helped, and kicking footholds. It took forever to scrabble and slide to the bottom.

He reached what was left of the carriage. Mathilda and the other horse were dead, necks broken, but he spared them scarcely a glance.

Penelope Bancroft sat in the wreckage, cradling her husband's head, rocking him, murmuring to him, sobs catching in her throat.

Even in the gloom as the fog swirled about them, Carlos could see that his master's eyes were open and staring. He was dead.

How she had survived was a miracle!

She was hurt, coughing and moaning as she rocked her husband. Carlos tried to take the body from her, but she resisted, hugging it closer, whispering softly to it.

"They shouldn't allow children out so late at night, W.R. You're going to have to talk to the mayor about a curfew for children. It just isn't right for them to jump out and scare horses that way."

Children? Carlos stared at her. Her mind had suffered, he realized. But children? The evening's events played through his head, and he recalled the dark shadows near the carriage, the twigs breaking, and the high-pitched giggles.

But he had not thought it a childish giggle! Where had he heard it before? Was it on the waterfront? From the Chinese coolies?

He stared up through the drifting mist at the edge of the cliff above them. It seemed to hang over them like doom. He looked back at his mistress and dead master. Was it possible the horse team had so easily broken through that heavy wooden barrier? He had never examined it closely, but its massive construction seemed to be ample assurance that no team would ever crash through to plunge over Dead Man's Drop.

Carlos had a fleeting memory that as he was thrown from the carriage box, the horse team had crashed through the thick fence as if it had been made of matchsticks! The heavy wood had splintered. Splintered!

5

It had shattered too easily. Carlos crossed himself. "Too easy," he said aloud in a hoarse voice. It had been no accident! He remembered now, something had spooked Mathilda! No—some*one* had spooked her, and it had been done deliberately. There had been darker shadows in the gloom, blending with the swirling mist. He shuddered, recalling the curious giggle.

His mistress must have seen something, too! She had whispered about children, and there were no children, of that he was certain. *How could a child do these things*? he thought.

No, it was his fault—his—Carlos's. If he had been paying attention to his driving, to guarding his passengers, none of this would have happened. His master would still be alive; Mr. and Mrs. Bancroft would now be home in bed, and all would be well.

But he, foolish man, had been too interested in things not his business—listening to the Bancrofts—to notice the warnings, the sounds and the shadows. He should have prevented the accident, he should have! He had caused his beloved master's death.

But was that true? He had not killed Señor Bancroft but someone had!

It was murder!

Carlos's first instinct was to explain to his mistress that it was no accident they were at the bottom of the cliff—that they were all supposed to have been killed. But he saw she would not understand.

Someone wanted them dead! Wanted the Bancrofts out of the way. And they had nearly succeeded. They had ended the life of one of San Francisco's wealthiest and most influential citizens. Someone had succeeded in snuffing out the life of the fifth member of the Silver Kings of the Comstock Lode. Señor Bancroft was dead.

Carlos swallowed hard and said nothing to his mistress. If she understood, it would only worry her.

She seemed to have no broken bones. She was scratched, and her clothing was torn, and some of her jewelry was missing, but she was whole. Only her mind seemed shattered. She continued to rock her husband and murmur to him.

Carlos thought in Spanish, *Is she in any further danger?*

6

Am I? He wondered if there would be someone waiting, ready to pounce and murder him as he tried to go for help for his mistress.

He looked around for his revolver. It had slipped from his grasp when he'd been thrown from the carriage. He found it at last in the weeds near the dead horses. He wiped off the dirt and shoved it into his belt. Well, if there were enemies to face, he would face them.

His mistress was probably doomed if he did not bring help soon. He went back to her, found a mohair blanket in the wreck, and draped it around her narrow shoulders. She did not seem to notice. He assured her that everything would be just fine. But if she heard his voice, she did not answer.

The easiest way to reach help was to climb on down the hill, find a street, and follow it to life and assistance.

He started out.

Chapter 2

Melissa Sue Bancroft woke from a deep sleep. She opened her eyes, blinking in the gloom; the room was still very dark. It must be very early. What was that dreadful pounding downstairs? Was someone at the front door? She could hear muffled shouts from outside the house.

Pushing out of bed, she donned a blue robe and fluffed her lustrous brown hair as she strode into the hall. Someone *was* pounding at the front door! What in the world?

She stood at the head of the curving double staircase, peering over the balustrade. She called to the butler: "Garfield!"

Was she the only one who had heard the noise? She looked round at the closed doors, surprised that her father, W.R., wasn't up, taking charge. A clatter as loud as that had never failed to wake him before. She took several steps down, calling again, "Garfield!"

"Here, Missy." Garfield, in a figured magenta robe, his stringy graying hair uncombed, hurried from the back of the house. He was followed by one of the maids and a cook, both half-dressed. Seeing Melissa, the women hung back, whispering to each other. Another maid joined them.

Melissa said, "See what that noise is. Have you seen my father?"

"No, Missy. He isn't back yet." Garfield, a wisp of a man who seemed even smaller when only partially dressed, went to the massive front door and peered through the large square peephole.

Mrs. Oglethorpe, the housekeeper, a stout gray-haired woman, came into the hall and looked up at Melissa on the stairs. "What is it, Miss Melissa?"

"I don't know." Her father and mother weren't back yet? How strange.

"Good heavens!" Garfield said suddenly, in great distress. He unbolted the door and flung it back. Carlos Ortega, looking as if he had been in a bloody fight, came in with three other men. The men were carrying someone on a litter.

Melissa ran down the stairs, her heart pounding, a feeling of dread inside her. "What happened!?"

"A terrible accident, Señorita," Carlos muttered. "Señora Bancroft is hurt—"

"Oh, no!" In terror, Melissa pulled the covering away and looked down at the face of her mother. The older woman was alive, but her face was scratched and bloody. She was deathly pale, and her breathing came in shallow gasps.

"Oh, my God!" Melissa turned, shouting for the maids to prepare her mother's bed. She pointed, "Take her upstairs." Then she looked around for the butler. "Garfield, send someone for Doctor Witherspoon at once!"

He nodded and hurried away.

Melissa gathered up her robe and ran up the steps after the men, her heart seeming to flutter. An accident!? Where was her father? She ran into the room. A maid had turned back the bed, and the men were gently putting her mother into it as the maid fussed.

Carlos motioned the men out and paused by the bedroom door. Melissa said to the maid, "Get some warm water—wash her face." She knelt by the bed, smoothing the sheets, then turned to Carlos. "Where's my father?"

Carlos mumbled something, edging away.

"Tell me. What happened?"

"There was an accident— The horses—"

"What about the horses?"

Carlos shifted uneasily under the young woman's stare. "I am so sorry, Señorita. . . . There was nothing anyone—"

9

She shook him. "Carlos! What happened?"

He moved into the hallway as the maid returned with a basin and towels. He said, "An accident, Señorita. Someone spooked the horses—"

"Someone? Who?"

"I don't know." Carlos shrugged elaborately. "It was dark, and the fog—"

"What happened to my father?"

"They—they—they took him away."

She shook him again. "Where, Carlos!? Where?"

The words came out of him as if by the roots. "To the undertaker's, Señorita."

Melissa released him and stepped back, her face a mask of horror. "Oh, my God! He is dead?"

Carlos nodded slowly, with great reluctance.

Melissa leaned against the wall, closing her eyes. "Oh, no, no, no—"

The maid came to the door. "Mrs. Bancroft is talking, Miss Melissa—"

Melissa roused herself with great effort. She looked at Carlos as if seeing him for the first time, his clothes dirty and torn, face scratched and pale. She took his hand. "I will come and talk with you in a moment, Carlos. . . ."

"Si, Señorita."

She went into the room and knelt again by the bed. Her mother was babbling, the words scarcely more than whispers. Melissa glanced around at the maid. "Bring some brandy, please."

"Yes, Miss." The servant hurried out.

Penelope Bancroft turned her head slightly, gazing at her daughter. "They should not be out so late."

"Who, Mother?"

"The children. We must speak to W.R. and see that he talks to the mayor. It is dangerous for children to be on the roads late at night."

"Of course it is, Mother. I will speak to him." Melissa wondered, *Whatever does she mean? Children? What children?*

"Melissa, love, you are a good daughter." Penelope tried to

10

reach out and could not. Melissa squeezed her hand.

"You must sleep now, Mother."

"Yes, I am tired . . . but I must tell your father good night."

"You're much too tired. I will tell him for you."

"Thank you, dear." Penelope closed her eyes.

Melissa stood, looking down at her mother. Her heart seemed like a rock inside her. What would they do now that W.R. was gone? It was almost impossible to imagine a time without him. He had always been there, if sometimes in the background. She had always known she could go to him. She had been her father's girl.

He had always said she was the image of her mother when Penelope was her age. They had the same large brown eyes with flecks of gold, the same hair and delicate skin, the same lovely oval face . . .

The maid returned with a decanter and a brandy snifter. Melissa took it and turned away from the bed. "Where's Doctor Witherspoon?"

"They sent for him, Miss."

Melissa sighed deeply. "Stay with her, Josie. I'm going to get dressed."

"Yes, Miss."

Melissa went out. Carlos was still in the hallway, waiting as she had asked. She gave him the decanter and the glass. "I think you need this . . ."

"*Gracias*, Señorita." He poured into the snifter.

"Now, tell me what happened."

Carlos sipped the brandy and related the events as they happened on the way back from the dinner party in the dense fog. The dark shadows and the frightened horses.

"Why did Mother talk about children?"

"I thought I heard somebody giggling, and she mus' have heard it, too."

"Giggling? That's odd. . . ."

"It happened very fast, Missy. And the wood fence—it broke too easy."

"The barrier? Those are very heavy beams!"

"But they broke like that!" Carlos snapped his fingers. He poured another drink.

11

Melissa stared at him. "Do you know what you're saying? Somebody sabotaged the barrier!"

"What does that mean, sabo—?"

"It means someone must have sawed the barrier so it would break easily."

Carlos nodded quickly. "Si, Missy. I think so, too."

"We must tell this to the police right away." Melissa turned, then paused. "Get some clean clothes, Carlos. Do you feel all right?"

"I am all right, Señorita." He shrugged sadly. "I was lucky. . . ."

Melissa was dressed when the family physician arrived. Dr. Witherspoon was a kindly looking middle-aged man with a white goatee and fluffy side whiskers. He came hurrying in with his black bag, and Melissa took him upstairs to her mother's room, explaining on the way that the older woman had been in an accident.

Witherspoon paused at the door and frowned at the young woman. "You say both your parents were in the carriage? Where is your father, then?"

She took a deep breath. "He is at the funeral parlor."

Witherspoon pressed his lips together. "I'm very sorry, Melissa . . . very sorry indeed."

Melissa opened the door to her mother's room.

Mrs. Oglethorpe assisted the physician as he made his examination, which took about an hour. Melissa sat downstairs, chewing her nails until Witherspoon came out, buttoning his coat and descending the stairs slowly to face her. She jumped to her feet.

"You must be brave, my dear."

"What did you find?"

"Your mother will probably never walk again. She has profound spinal damage and must be moved only with extreme care."

Melissa dropped into a chair, closing her eyes. She bowed her head and bit her lower lip hard. She must be strong. She was the only Bancroft now—until her brother, Worthy, arrived home from the East. She must wire him at once.

"In my opinion," Witherspoon said, "your mother will probably be bedridden permanently."

"Does she have other injuries?"

The physician nodded slowly. "I cannot tell the extent of her internal injuries, of course. Only time will tell us that."

Melissa nodded, then shook her head.

"She fell with the carriage from a great height?"

"Yes, from Dead Man's Drop."

"Then it's a miracle she survived at all. There are many things we cannot explain." He handed her a slip of paper. "This is the medicine she must take. I will come every day to look at her. I understand the driver was also injured?"

"Yes, but he says he is all right. He was thrown clear and did not fall far."

"I see." Witherspoon went to the door, motioning Melissa to remain seated. He made a little bow. "I will see you tomorrow then, Melissa."

"Thank you, doctor." She watched him open the door and go out.

Worthy. I must wire Worthy at once.

At the sitting room desk, she composed a wire and gave it to Garfield. "Have someone take this to the nearest telegraph office and send it immediately."

"Yes, Miss Melissa. If I may, what did the doctor say about Mrs. Bancroft?"

Melissa swallowed hard. "My mother will be bedridden, I'm afraid. The doctor fears she will never walk again. Please ask Mrs. Oglethorpe to see to it that one of the maids stays with her at all times."

"I will. If I may, Miss Melissa, I would like to express my deep sorrow at this tragedy."

"Thank you, Garfield."

Melissa went into the drawing room to be alone. It was a strange feeling to be in charge of the household. Her mother had always been so efficient, she had never given the running of the house a thought. Now, so suddenly, everything would change. Somewhere she must find the courage and the good sense to take charge. She was only nineteen.... But in some families, she knew, nineteen was almost ancient. She took a

13

long, deep breath. She could do it. She would have to do it—until Worthy came home.

Garfield summoned Melissa. "The police have arrived, Missy."

There were two men in the foyer, one in uniform. The man in plain clothes was the younger and introduced himself as Inspector Ambrose Jenkins.

"And this is Sergeant Horace Riley, Miss Bancroft."

Melissa nodded. She had forgotten about the police and hadn't given them a thought since the doctor came . . . but, of course, they would want to know about her father's death.

"I'm terribly sorry about your father, Miss Bancroft. I knew him personally. He was a fine man—an exceptional man, if I may say so. The city will miss him a great deal."

"Thank you, Inspector." Jenkins was a well-dressed man in his forties; he sported a black mustache and wore a herringbone suit with a gold pin in his lapel. In contrast, the sergeant appeared almost shabby, his uniform wrinkled and stained in places. He was probably ten years older than his superior, she thought, with a rather hard face—an unforgiving face.

Jenkins said, "May we speak to your mother, Miss Bancroft?"

"She's asleep. The doctor gave her something to let her rest. She had a terrifying ordeal—"

"Um, yes. Of course." Jenkins consulted a bit of yellow paper. "Your driver is a man named Carlos Ortega, is he not?"

"Yes."

"May we ask him a few questions, please?"

Melissa nodded. "I'll send for him. Won't you both have a seat?" She indicated the sitting room.

She rang for Garfield, who arrived almost immediately, as if just waiting to be summoned. "Will you ask Carlos to come to the sitting room, please? The police want to ask him about the accident."

"Yes. Certainly, Miss Melissa." Garfield hurried out.

Melissa assured them, "He should be here in a few moments. He's probably at the stables."

Jenkins nodded. "How long has he been with you?"

14

"Ever so long—he's like one of the family. I've known him and his wife all my life."

"Oh, so he's married, is he?"

"Oh, yes. He and Juanita, his wife, have an apartment over the stables."

"Did he tell you what had happened?"

Melissa looked surprised. "Of course. He felt miserable about it. He was the one who went for help."

Jenkins nodded again, and the sergeant seemed to glare at her. She ignored him. Beside Jenkins, he was a ruffian.

In another moment, Garfield reappeared. "Miss Melissa, I'm afraid we cannot locate Carlos."

"Why not?" Jenkins demanded.

"I don't know, sir." Garfield was on the point of wringing his hands. "He isn't anywhere on the premises. He must have gone somewhere. Perhaps to the doctor."

The sergeant growled, and Jenkins said, "Let's talk to his wife. What's her name again?"

"Juanita, sir," Garfield quaked.

Melissa said to Garfield, "Please ask Juanita to come in."

Relieved, the old man nodded and hurried away.

Melissa said, "Juanita has been with us for ages. She was our nanny when we were small—"

"Who's 'we'?"

"My brother Worthy and me."

Jenkins said, "Oh, yes. I've met Worthington, Junior. You call him Worthy?"

"Yes."

"Where is he? Why isn't he here?"

"He's in Boston. I've sent him a wire."

"Very good."

Jenkins rose and paced the room until Juanita appeared. She was a stout middle-aged woman wearing a flowered dress. She seemed very nervous, looking to Melissa.

Melissa said, "Juanita, these policemen want to ask you—"

Jenkins interrupted, demanding, "Where is your husband?"

Juanita shook her head quickly: "I am sorry. I do not know."

15

"You do not know!?" Jenkins took a step toward her.

"Please, Señor, I 'ave not seen him." She backed up a step.

Jenkins's manner said he did not believe her. With exaggerated politeness, he said, "When did you see him last, Señora Ortega?"

Juanita looked from him to Melissa and back. "When he drove Señor Bancroft and—"

"That was hours ago!" the sergeant growled. "Tell us the truth!"

"Señor, it *is* the truth!"

"You don't have to badger her!" Melissa said hotly. She went to stand by the older woman.

Jenkins said icily, "Ortega drove his employers—your parents—off a cliff, and now he has disappeared. Doesn't that look strange to you, Miss Bancroft?"

Melissa reacted in horror. "You cannot believe that he—"

Jenkins pointed his finger at her. "In my work, Miss Bancroft, the obvious is usually true. I think Ortega killed your parents."

Chapter 3

Melissa stood at the front door, watching the two policemen stride away down the walk to the street. It was outrageous that they believed Carlos had killed her father and maimed her mother!

She closed the door and went back to face Juanita. "You really don't know where he is?"

The woman shook her head tearfully. "I 'ave not seen him. I was asleep when he came back with . . ." She paused in confusion.

"Where would he go?"

She shook her head again and shrugged her chubby shoulders. "Many places."

Melissa hugged her. "All right. If you hear from him, please let me know. I will say nothing."

The young woman went back to her bedroom suite and stood by a window looking out. Inspector Jenkins had said they would be back and a search would be instituted to find Carlos. It was nonsense to think that Carlos had anything to do with the death of her father.

Sighing, she sat at her writing desk, thinking about Worthy. He would be shocked to hear the news. There should be a wire from him at any moment, explaining that he was returning home at once.

Idly Melissa picked up an envelope and looked at the bold

17

handwriting on the address. It was from Jessica Starbuck, her school chum. She had not seen Jessie for years, but they still corresponded. Jessie was always traveling around the country, helping out people who had problems. She was not sure exactly what Jessie did—some sort of investigative business, she gathered from her letters. Of course, with such a wealthy father as the late Alex Starbuck, Jessie led an exciting life. She must write to Jessie soon.

She changed clothes with a heavy heart. She must go to the funeral parlor and see about the arrangements. God, she wished Worthy were here. Worthy was older and very capable. She thought of him as being able to do almost anything he set his mind to.

She went downstairs and asked Garfield to have one of the older stablehands bring a light carriage around to the side door.

They would not allow her to view her father's body. Melissa wept, standing by the casket, until they led her away. She composed herself in a tiny mourning room, then completed the arrangements, signed the papers, and was driven home again.

There was a telegram from Worthy waiting for her. He was indeed shocked and saddened at his father's death and would take the next train. She could expect him in about ten days, depending on the weather, the railroad, and the vagaries of travel.

She sat at her desk with the wire and began to feel much better. No matter what happened, Worthy would know how to handle it. But ten days was a long time. . . .

Inspector Jenkins returned later in the day, demanding to talk to her mother. "She is our only witness, Miss Bancroft"—he gave her a stern look—"until we find Ortega."

Melissa sighed. "My mother has sustained severe injuries, Inspector. She has been through a dreadful ordeal, and the shock has made her incoherent. You will not be able to question her."

"I will be the judge of that." He motioned toward the stairs. "I insist on seeing her."

Annoyed, Melissa led the way upstairs. Jenkins went into the room as the maid looked at Melissa in surprise. The policeman stood over the bed, staring down at the frail older woman.

"Is she awake?"

The maid nodded. "I think so, sir."

Jenkins said, "Mrs. Bancroft . . ."

Penelope Bancroft turned her head slightly and opened her eyes. "Oh, there you are, W.R. I wanted to show you my new gown."

Jenkins frowned at her and looked at Melissa. "Who does she think I am?"

"She called my father W.R."

Mrs. Bancroft said, "Josie, bring the new gown for Mr. Bancroft to see."

Jenkins retreated, blowing out his breath. The maid went to the bedside.

In the hallway with the door closed, Melissa vented her anger. "Are you satisfied we're not lying to you, Inspector!"

"I had to find out!"

"My father was murdered—and not by Carlos! Why won't you listen? Someone killed my father and paralyzed my mother! If you weren't so ready to clap Carlos into jail, I know he would tell you all he knows."

"If he's so innocent, why doesn't he come forward?"

"Because he's afraid you will try him and hang him without listening to what he has to say. And I don't blame him."

Jenkins smiled patronizingly. "I believe you are hiding him, Miss Bancroft. I assure you, it will go hard with you if I can prove it. Your standing in this city will not protect you if you are hiding a murderer."

Melissa closed her eyes, sighing deeply. "Why won't you believe us? Carlos is no more a murderer than I am." She stared at him intently. "You are the fool, Inspector. You refuse to see the truth."

Jenkins controlled his anger. "My dear young lady. We believe Carlos Ortega is saving his own hide. He was careless and irresponsible at the very least. If it was not murder, it was something very like it. And to cover up his criminal negligence, he makes up the story he told you about someone who giggled chasing the team and carriage off the cliff."

"What about the barrier? It splintered!"

"We have found no evidence of a saw cut. I'm sorry, Miss Bancroft, but Ortega is our number one suspect. I advise you to tell him to give himself up. If he does not, we will hunt him down, and it will go doubly hard on him when we do. Every policeman in San Francisco will be looking for him by morning."

"Carlos did not lie to me," she said dully.

He shrugged. "You are free to believe what you will."

"Carlos has been with our family since before I was born." She glared at him. "I would take his word over yours any day."

He took a breath, stared at her, and turned on his heel.

Melissa watched him leave, slamming the front door behind him. His mind was made up. She would get nowhere with him. Probably he and others like him hoped they would find Carlos and that he would try to run. Then they would have an excuse to shoot to kill. They had already pegged him as a criminal.

Where is Carlos? she wondered.

She went back upstairs and reread Worthy's telegram. "Oh, hurry, please!" she said aloud. She felt so alone. Never before had she had the managing of affairs on her slender shoulders. She was unaccustomed to it, and the situation frightened her.

Why were the police afraid of the truth? She bit her lip, thinking about the truth. Who in the world would want her parents dead? Several times at the dinner table, she had heard her father discuss police corruption. Was it possible the police themselves had killed him? What a horrid idea!

If he were here now, Worthy would make them sit up and take notice, she thought. *My brother would stand firm and make them do something. And he would believe Carlos.* She sighed, knowing they would take Worthy much more seriously than they did her—a young debutante fresh from her cotillion. Older, wiser, and bearing the family name—Worthington Ralston Bancroft, Jr.—Worthy always commanded respect.

She picked up the envelope with Jessie Starbuck's letter in it, looking at it, her forehead furrowed. Could Jessie help? In another letter, Jessie had mentioned how she and her companion Ki had helped people. . . .

Making up her mind suddenly, Melissa took a pen and began to write.

When she finished, she took the letter downstairs and rang for Garfield. She gave him the letter, asking him to post it immediately. Writing the letter made her feel much better all of a sudden. It was action—she had done something. Worthy would be proud of her.

Josiah Kelton came into the office room and slammed the door. The huge, gold-figured mirror on the wall beside the doorway rocked and slewed sideways. He strode to his desk and pounded a fist on it with such force that the papers and the heavy quartz paperweight bounced.

Two small Chinese men facing him, perched on the edge of their chairs like robins ready to take flight, quaked in terror.

Kelton shouted at them, "You stupid coolies botched the job!" He leaned over the desk as if they hadn't heard him. "You are a couple of horse turds! You cannot do the simplest thing! They were all supposed to die!"

Kelton was a short, husky man. Seemingly all muscle, his coat bulged and threatened to rip at the seams. His face was crimson in his rage, and his fist pounded the desk again as the two Orientals jumped. His voice was like the roar of a wounded animal, and his tiny dark eyes bored into them.

"There should have been no survivors to testify! This is going to cost me a pretty penny to cover up! Because you were stupid! Everything was figured for you! You cannot do the simplest thing! I ought to sell your wives on the open market and send you two back to China!"

The two hapless Chinese shifted and agonized. Sell their wives!? They said nothing at all—trying to pretend they did not understand—but they knew he was aware they spoke enough English to hear his words.

Kelton pounded the desk again and yelled at them to leave. "Get out of my sight!"

The two Asians scurried to the door, and Kelton threw the paperweight at them. It smashed the door panel, and the two squeaked, running and jabbering as they left the room. Kelton dropped into a chair, muttering to himself. He was surrounded by idiots! Now there was a witness who could point the finger at him through those stupid coolies. His plan had been well worked out; the entire thing would have seemed a tragic accident in the fog.

And now Ortega was alive. *Damn!* The old woman had survived, too, but she knew nothing—so he was informed. He had his informants.

One of them would bring him news of Ortega. . . .

Chapter 4

Jessica Starbuck was surprised to receive a reply from Melissa Bancroft so soon. Usually Melissa forgot to write and had a hundred explanations why she was tardy in answering. This time the letter came swiftly.

Jessica and Ki were in Carson City, Nevada, not far from San Francisco, enjoying a well-earned rest.

"Oh, dear," she said, "W.R. is dead."

"Who is W.R.?"

"My friend Melissa Bancroft's father. In her letter she says he was murdered. I knew him a long time ago. He was a leader in San Francisco, and I suppose he had a few enemies." Jessie sighed. "Melissa accuses a man named Josiah Kelton. And I'm sure she has not a shred of evidence to back up her claim."

Ki smiled. "What sort of person is Melissa?"

"Very like her mother, honest and fair. Maybe too much so at times. She does tend to jump to conclusions."

"Maybe she's doing that now."

Jessie made a face. "Well, her father *is* dead. According to her, the accident was no accident at all. But the police think otherwise."

Ki said, "The police should be better informed on murder than a young woman."

"Yes, I agree, but there have been rumors about the San

Francisco police, linking them with corruption in high places. You've heard of the Broderick machine, haven't you? It's just possible she may be right."

Ki smiled broadly. "And you're going to see what you can do to help."

Jessie smiled back. "You just read my mind. I'm going to wire Silas Dent right now. We'll need his help."

"Is he back in San Francisco?"

"He never really left. He just set up shop in Wyoming to capitalize on the Gold Rush. He'll be our ace in the hole. Are you coming along?"

"I wouldn't let you go alone."

Josiah Kelton sent for Zack and Grady, his best hired guns. When they arrived, he took them into the office and locked the door. Zack was lean and dark, slightly stooped, usually wearing rumpled clothes. He seemed to take pleasure in looking like anything but a dandy. He was a knife man.

Grady was heavier, with thick shoulders and a stubby nose that had been broken several times. Neither man would qualify as a genius, Kelton knew, but they could obey specific instructions.

Kelton faced them. "You heard that W.R. Bancroft got himself killed?"

They both nodded. "Yeah, we heard."

"Well, there's one more Bancroft who could really cause trouble."

"You mean the girl?" Grady asked.

"No, I mean the brother. His name is Worthington. He must be about twenty-four now. He's in Boston and probably getting on a train right now to come West." Kelton opened his desk drawer and fished in it, bringing out a copy of an Eastern magazine. Flipping through it, he said, "This is a picture of him," and shoved it across the desk.

Grady grabbed it. "He looks like one of them fancy Eastern dudes."

Kelton sat back and lighted a cigar. "He isn't as soft as he looks." He puffed on the cigar for a moment, then pointed it at them. "I don't want him to arrive here. You understand me?"

Both men nodded. Zack studied the picture. "He looks like his old man."

Kelton rose. "He'll probably come in on the train, but he might get off at Sacramento and take the stagecoach from there. So you'll have to watch both depots."

Grady asked, "Why would he get off in Sacramento?"

"Because he's not dumb, for crissakes. His sister has told him that his old man was murdered. He might figure he's next."

"Ohhh." Grady nodded and tucked the magazine into his pocket. He turned and shoved Zack toward the door.

Kelton said, "You go down to the depot and find out when his train would get in if he gets on the first train out of Boston today."

"Sure, boss."

Kelton sat down again as the two closed the door behind them. He felt rather satisfied with himself. He'd had the foresight to bribe a couple of employees in the telegraph offices to bring him copies of every wire sent and received by the Bancroft household. He sighed, thinking it was too bad he could not bribe someone at the post office, too.

He had put the word out about Carlos Ortega. He was offering money for information about him, and even more money for his body. Kelton had made it clear—he did not want the man alive.

Now all he could do was wait.

He was puffing on his cigar, staring at the opposite wall, when he heard the ruckus. *What the hell!?*

Kelton got up and strode into the hallway. The noise was coming from one of the gambling rooms. He leaned over the rail and called to Zack and Grady, who were nearing the bottom of the stairs. He motioned them back up.

Kelton opened the door to the gambling room. A youngish man was shouting at a poker dealer, and Kelton recognized him as Ralph Hickson, a young punk with more money than brains. Hickson was yelling that the game was fixed and that he had been cheated out of five thousand dollars.

Zack and Grady ran past Kelton and converged on young Hickson, who instantly pulled a pistol.

The dealer faded away, and Zack warned, "Look out, he's got a gun!" He made a feint at Hickson. The young man fired well over his head, and Grady shot him three times. Hickson collapsed over the poker table, crashing to the floor. Zack leaned down, feeling for a pulse. There was none.

Kelton watched from the doorway for a moment, then went back to his office. They would handle it. What the hell was one young kid?

Zack searched the body and pocketed the small roll of bills he found. "I'll see his family gets it." Someone laughed. He motioned two waiters to come and carry the body downstairs. They would send a boy for the undertaker.

A messenger came to the saloon with a sealed note for Josiah Kelton, and one of the bartenders brought it upstairs to the office.

Kelton closed the door behind the man and tore open the envelope. It was an unsigned note, but he was sure he knew who it was from. It was a warning that Kelton's business with W.R. Bancroft was too open, and the murder all but transparent. Kelton growled at that. *Those goddamn coolies!*

But what was worse, the sender wanted money. It was necessary to keep things covered up and to pad law enforcement pockets, so what was a little more? But that didn't make it any easier to swallow.

Kelton wadded up the note and hurled it across the room, shouting, "You bloodsucking sonofabitch! I'm not gonna forget this!" He kicked a chair out of his way and screamed to the ceiling, "Those goddamn coolies! They did this to me!"

Melissa was awakened by Mrs. Oglethorpe late at night. The young woman opened her eyes, blinking at the candle on the nightstand.

The housekeeper said, "Missy, get up. Carlos is downstairs."

"Carlos!"

"I put him in the pantry."

"Good." She slid out of bed and pulled a robe about her. "Does anyone else know he's here?"

26

"Garfield knows. . . ." Mrs. Oglethorpe took up the candle. "He came to Garfield's window." She went ahead to light the way.

Carlos was frightened. "I am afraid for my life, Señorita! They gonna hang me if they find me!"

"Well, they certainly are not!"

"Señorita, they won't gi' me a chance! This I know." He was dressed in the same torn clothes he'd been wearing at the time of the accident. He needed a shave and looked very worn. Melissa had never seen him this way.

"Where have you been staying?"

"With friends. They hide me. But I am afraid if they catch me there, they hurt them, too."

It was a very real worry, she thought, recalling the sergeant—what was his name—Riley. "We must think of a better place for you to hide." She looked around for Garfield.

Carlos said quickly, "I cannot stay here, Señorita. They gonna search this place every now 'n' then. I know this."

Melissa knew this was probably true. Garfield was not in the room, and she was about to ask Mrs. Oglethorpe to go fetch him when he returned in a hurry.

"The police are outside, Miss Melissa!" Garfield said in alarm. "They must have seen Carlos come in!"

"They watch the house," Carlos said, groaning.

In the next moment, there was a pounding at the front door.

Melissa said, "Garfield, take your time opening the door. Then talk to them—anything—" As the servant ran out, she turned to Carlos. "Come this way."

She led him toward the back of the house, then down a flight of steep stairs to the basement. She and Worthy had crawled in and out of the cellar windows when they were children, and no one had ever been able to figure out how they came and went.

With Carlos's help, she pushed open the window that led into heavy bushes. "Don't show yourself," she said. "Do you need money?"

He shrugged. "I got none, Señorita."

"All right. I have nothing with me now, but I'll send Garfield to the old market south of Mission Street tomorrow. Look for him there. Do you think you can?"

"I think so, Señorita. Gracias!"

"Garfield will go there in the morning before midday."

Carlos nodded and slid through the window.

Someone inside the house was shouting. Melissa pushed him hard. "Go! But be careful!" She caught her breath as she watched him crawl away through the bushes. She thought, *What a silly thing to say!* But she hadn't been able to think of anything else. Of course, he'd be careful.

She stayed by the open window after Carlos was out of sight, holding her breath and biting her lip, listening. She and Worthy had played games here, but this was real! And what was worse, she was evading the law, actually breaking the law, by hiding Carlos. But there was nothing else she could do. She *had* to protect him as much as she could.

When she didn't hear any sounds of alarm, she thought he must be out of police reach. She closed the window and went back upstairs to confront a red-faced Inspector Jenkins.

"Where have you hidden him!"

Melissa smiled at him. "Have you searched the house, Inspector?"

"We're doing that now!"

"Then you won't need me." She turned. "Garfield, show these gentlemen out when they've finished."

"Yes, Miss Melissa," the butler said, trying not to smile.

Jenkins was fuming, and Melissa knew he was staring at her as she went up the staircase to her bedchamber. It was quite a thrill to have outfoxed him.

But it also made her more sure than ever that her father had been murdered. Was Jenkins on the payroll of whoever paid to have her father killed?

In the morning, Melissa gave Garfield an envelope of money to give to Carlos and sent him off to the old market well south of Mission Street on the far side of town. The butler was to purchase fresh vegetables and certain spices unobtainable in the newer, more anglicized, markets nearby.

She thought Garfield, too, rather enjoyed eluding the police. His step seemed more spritely as he went out.

She dressed, called for a carriage, and was driven to the central police station. There she asked to speak with the Chief of Police, Harlan Granville. He was an old family friend.

His aide told her the chief was out of town.

She called on the mayor, Cloyd Kimball, who used to dandle her on his knee. His aide expressed sorrow, but the mayor was unable to fit her into his schedule. Perhaps another time . . .

She firmed her jaw and went to see Councilman Farley Crafts, also a close family friend. He was in court, they told her. If she would care to make an appointment . . .

As she left the councilman's office, Bert Hutchinson took her arm. "Melissa, you must go home. You're accomplishing nothing here."

"I know that all too well!"

An attorney, Hutchinson was a dear friend of her father. He pulled her into an alcove and lowered his voice. "Go home, and I will relay you any information I can elicit. Do you know where the man Ortega is?"

"No, I don't," she said in all honesty.

He nodded. "Your case rests on his testimony if he ever gets on the stand."

"That's what I'm afraid of—that they'll kill him before he can tell what he knows in court."

"A very real fear, my dear," Hutchinson said.

Chapter 5

Melissa stood in the church, surrounded by her father's friends, Garfield and the household staff. Mrs. Oglethorpe had ready handkerchiefs and a firm grip on her elbow.

The casket, carved wood and polished brass, heaped with flowers, was a dozen feet in front of her at the altar. There were bowers and sprays of flowers everywhere. The mayor, chief of police, and most of the councilmen were there. All the foremost citizens of San Francisco had turned out, as well as some of very modest means who W.R. had helped out in their time of need.

Everyone listened to the eulogy, then crowded around Melissa. She heard their condolences, a patter like water splashing over a spillway. She could not distinguish one from another.

She pushed through the other mourners finally, with Mrs. Oglethorpe cutting a path, and reached her carriage. The mayor had been impossible to reach yesterday; but today, in public, he was all soft and soothing words. She sank back on the cushions of the carriage and closed her eyes.

The funeral procession went along Van Ness, halting all other traffic as it turned west on California Street and up the hill to the cemetery. Melissa thought of her brother. Worthy would be distressed that he'd missed the funeral, but she knew he would not expect them to wait until he finally arrived. She was surprised at the massive turnout, though the newspapers had devoted a full front-page column and another half-page inside to W.R.'s obituary—recounting his exploits, starting with his days as a prospector. He had been one of a partnership then and had risen to great wealth and power in The City.

She was glad her mother had no inkling of the funeral; it would only worsen her condition. Melissa had given strict orders that no matter what, Mrs. Bancroft was not to be told W.R. was dead.

The procession turned in at the cemetery, and her carriage stopped near the open grave. Mrs. Oglethorpe and Garfield helped her down. Juanita was close by, looking very sad. Melissa took her hand. A man in black with a Bible in his hand loomed up, and Melissa paused, listening to his condolences. She nodded. Then she saw Josiah Kelton and stared at him in astonishment. He dared to come here! He was with an overdressed woman in a low-cut gown. She must be his mistress, Carlotta. *How inappropriate!* she thought.

Melissa pulled her eyes away from them and took her place by the gravesite, leaning against Mrs. Oglethorpe's comforting bulk. The preacher droned on; someone handed her a flower from the casket; and the ceremony was over.

Mrs. Oglethorpe said, "Let's go home now, Missy."

Carlos Ortega read in the papers that W.R.'s funeral was to be held the next day. He must attend. Señor Bancroft may have been his employer for many years, but he was also a very good friend. The señor had come up the hard way, by his bootstraps, and knew what it was to be hungry or an outcast. He had treated Carlos as a man, with respect.

Of course, Carlos knew that if he attended the funeral, he would be arrested and thrown in jail—or worse.

He must disguise himself. The police had no picture of him. He had never in his life had one taken, not even at his wedding. They only had a description, and he was certain he looked like a thousand others.

But he *was* Mexican, and that could not be hidden easily. If he showed up at the funeral, one Mexican in a crowd of Anglos, he would stand out.

31

But he could go and pretend to be putting flowers on a nearby grave. Señor Bancroft would understand.

When the time came, Carlos dressed in his best, bought flowers, and hurried to the cemetery. He was kneeling not far from the open grave when the procession arrived. He tried not to look at them—a few quick glances—Juanita was there, close by Señorita Melissa. He gritted his teeth, wanting to go and comfort her.

He could hear the preacher quite clearly, and tears came to his eyes for Señor Bancroft. The ceremony was almost over when he turned his head and looked directly into Juanita's eyes!

He could almost hear her gasp from where he was kneeling.

But others, closer, did hear it. As the ceremony concluded, Chief Granville gave hurried orders, and Carlos saw uniformed men converging on him. He had underestimated the police! They had been watching Juanita, too!

He had to run. He had a dozen yards head start on them, but he heard them yell and saw drivers from the many carriages hurry to cut him off. He swerved, jumping over headstones and rushing slightly downhill toward the distant houses,

Someone fired at him, and the bullet caromed off a marble crypt, showering him with bits of stone. Carlos ducked away and heard the men shout that he was hit.

But he was losing them. He hurtled a hedge and ran across an expanse of grass, coming up against a tall board fence. Glancing back, he saw the closest man probably fifty yards behind him. He jumped, caught the top of the fence, pulled himself up and over, and fell into a garden.

He was conscious that several more shots had come seeking him out, but he could ignore them now. He ran between two houses, gained the street, and loped downhill. In another moment, he turned at a corner and slowed to a walk amid traffic.

In an hour, he was safe in his friend's home.

Melissa held on to the side of the carriage, hearing the police shout that Carlos Ortega was close by. Juanita was in tears, screaming, "He should not have come here! He should not have come!"

A cold hand gripped Melissa's heart as the police fired at the fleeing man, but she knew a running man is hard to hit. She had learned this from target shooting with her father. She tried to console Juanita, saying, "They will not catch him."

And they did not. They came straggling back in half an hour to say Carlos had eluded them. Chief Granville was disgusted. Melissa almost smiled as he glared at her as if she had something to do with it. Then she got into the carriage with Juanita and the others, and they went clattering off to the Bancroft mansion.

Juanita was mollified; they had not caught Carlos. But someone had yelled that he was hit.

"He could not be," Melissa told her, "or they would have caught him. Don't you see, they only thought he was hit." She could tell that the older woman felt better.

Jessica Starbuck and Ki took the stagecoach and arrived in San Francisco late in the evening, each apparently traveling alone. Jessica stepped down first, turning all heads. She was a honey-blonde, green-eyed young woman dressed in the latest lavender Paris fashion. Her ample breasts bobbed pleasantly as she stepped off the stage, and no man within sight of her noticed the tall man who was the last one off.

Jessie had no trouble getting a hack to take her to her hotel; half a dozen men rushed to do her bidding, to see her safely into the hack. Dressed casually in black jeans, shirt, and leather vest, Ki took another hack without assistance.

Ki, some thought, might have been an Indian, but he wasn't. He might have been Chinese, but he looked nothing like the Chinese laborers people saw in the streets. He was a puzzle to most.

Ki went directly to the office of Silas Dent, who would provide Jessica and him with anything they needed—information most of all. Silas had once worked for Jessica's father. Starting as a warehouseman many years ago, he was now known as *the* man to see in San Francisco, no matter what you wanted. If it was legal.

33

He kept his hand in politics as well and probably knew more about the Bancrofts and Kelton than anyone.

Jessie checked in at the Palace Hotel and then sent a message to Melissa.

By return messenger, Melissa urged her to come to the house at once: "I can't wait to see you!"

Jessica changed from her traveling clothes, slipping into a simple dark green Paris frock and pulling a matching cloak about her shoulders. The Palace doorman brought her a hack, and she rode at once to the Bancroft mansion.

Melissa came running down the steps to embrace her. "Jessie, you look wonderful!"

Garfield had food and drinks waiting for them in the parlor. The two young women chatted lightly at first.

"What an exciting day!" Melissa said happily. "I feel that my troubles are over with you here."

"What *are* your troubles?"

Melissa related all that had happened, including what Carlos had told her about the accident not being an accident and her reception at the police station and at city hall.

"Very curious," Jessica said. "And who do you think is behind all this?"

"I think it's Josiah Kelton. I know my father was having trouble with him and was trying to come to terms. I think Kelton solved the problem by having Father killed."

"Where's your brother? He isn't here?"

"Worthy was in Boston when it all happened. I wired him, and he's coming here at once." Melissa asked curiously, "Weren't you working with someone?"

"Yes. Ki is with me. He went to see someone as soon as we got off the stage. What kind of troubles was W.R. having?"

"I'm afraid I don't know any details."

"Were any threats made?"

"Melissa shrugged in a helpless gesture. "I don't know. My father never confided things like that to us."

Jessica nodded. She sipped the coffee Garfield had poured. "Would you like Ki and me to look into this for you?"

34

"Oh, would you!?"

Jessica smiled. "Of course. In fact, that's the reason we're here. Your situation is just a little too close to home. Remember, my father was murdered, too. Ki and I will do everything we can to bring W.R.'s killers to justice. We're at your disposal. Hopefully, this'll be a lot easier than solving my father's case."

Melissa said nothing.

For a brief instant, Jessica's face reflected the pain she still felt. Just as quickly, the look vanished, and she was all business. "We'll see what we can turn up. If there is a murderer here, we'll find him. We'll need names and addresses—"

"Yes. I'll get them."

"You said Garfield met with Carlos yesterday morning. I'd like to talk with Garfield about that first. Then I want to speak to every member of the staff. Someone may know something without knowing it. But first, Garfield?"

"I'll get him for you." Melissa rose and pulled the bell cord.

Garfield appeared in a few moments. "More coffee, Miss Melissa?"

Melissa said, "Not yet, thank you. Miss Starbuck here is a dear friend, Garfield. Please tell her what you told me about your meeting with Carlos."

Garfield nodded. "We met at the old market on the opposite side of town just as it had been arranged. After we made sure I had not been followed, I gave him the money Miss Melissa gave me in the envelope. He was most appreciative and quite fearful. He said he was staying with a good friend who lived near the waterfront. He was fairly sure he would be safe there for the time being, but he was extremely worried about his wife."

"Did you make arrangements to meet him again?"

"Yes, miss. I told him I would be back at the old market in four days."

"Good. Did you make any plan for contacting him sooner, in case of emergency?"

"No, miss." Garfield sounded crestfallen and glanced at Melissa.

"I'm sorry, I didn't think to plan for emergencies. . . . I guess I—" said Melissa.

"That's all right," Jessica said, smiling at them both reassuringly. "You did fine—for amateurs."

Melissa said proudly, "We have a conspiracy going."

"That may be, Melissa, but please do not get carried away with it," Jessica admonished soberly. To Garfield, she said, "Be very, very careful."

"I will be, miss. Very careful indeed," Garfield promised. He went out.

Jessica said, "I'm going to move in here with you. An old school chum come to console her dear young friend Missy in her bereavement and to visit her old sweetheart Worthy again. It would be best if I posed as Worthy's old girlfriend, since I am closer in age to him than to you. This plan would give me ample excuse to stay here without arousing suspicion."

Melissa smiled and nodded in agreement, her heart beating quickly as she began to understand her friend's plan. She had always admired and looked up to Jessica, not just because Jessie was older, but because Jessie had always been so capable and wise.

"Ki is getting a place to stay somewhere in town. No one must know he and I are together. I'm sure the police are watching this house for Carlos, and for all we know, the murderer is also having the house watched. I will get word to Ki, and he can come to us at night to work out our strategy."

"Who is Ki? Besides your partner I mean."

"He's my closest friend. A long time ago, he promised my father he would always take care of me. You'll like him when you meet him. You might even consider him exotic. He's very tall and well put together. An interesting blend of East and West. He's half-Japanese and half-American. Most women find him extremely attractive; most men find him intimidating. He needs no weapons to better most men."

"I must meet him. What's his full name?"

"Ki is all he wants to be known by. He will be here soon enough. Once I get a message to him, he'll slip in through the police surveillance."

"I know just the way for him to get in and out without

being seen." Melissa told Jessica about the window in the basement.

"To throw off the police, or anyone else keeping an eye on this place, let's drive over to the hotel and bring most of my bags back here. I want to make it look as if I have left the hotel."

Melissa looked puzzled. "Yes, but—"

"I want anyone watching this house to believe I am merely a house guest and no one to fear. But I need a place I can use as my headquarters. My father was a stockholder in the Palace Hotel, so the management will go along with anything I wish. I'm going to try to stay with you as much as possible. But when I'm not with you, I don't want you taking any chances by yourself. Don't go out alone; don't go out at night; and be very careful who you let in this house."

"I understand." Melissa paused. "Jessie, do you really think I may be in danger?"

"It's very possible."

Chapter 6

Worthington Ralston Bancroft, Jr., called Worthy since birth, was extremely frustrated. Thousands of miles from his mother and sister when they needed him the most, his father dead under mysterious circumstances. It was all a terrible blow! He found it almost impossible to imagine a world without W.R. Bancroft.

He wired Melissa at once that he was returning by the first train; then he packed his belongings and rushed for the depot.

On the train, it was difficult for him to sit still. He paced the car, went from one car to the next and back again, and even tried to get to the engine cab to insist the engineer make the train go faster.

It took forever to get to Chicago.

But finally the town showed up. He would have to change trains, and the next train west did not leave until morning. There was a hotel a long block from the station. He hailed a hack, his impatience still evident.

There was considerable traffic. It was late afternoon, and wagons, hacks, and buggies crowded the street. The hack had gone only half a block before Worthy noticed the two men in the open buggy next to him. One was driving, and he pulled their buggy up as close as possible to the slow-moving hack.

Worthy had taken notice of the two men because the man in the passenger seat was so intent on him. He could not seem to take his eyes off Worthy. The passenger was bearded, wearing black clothes and a beaver hat.

Worthy thought the passenger was about to shout at him, but instead the man pulled a pistol from under his coat and pointed it at him!

Worthy yelled to the hack driver and ducked as the first shot tore through the top of the hack. He heard the gunman swearing as the second shot slammed into metal and whined into the sky.

The hack driver hollered, "What the goddamn hell!" and slapped his reins so the horse reared. The hack swerved, and a third shot smashed into the rear seat.

Others were shouting now, alarmed by the shots; and Worthy peeked over the door top to see the buggy moving off rapidly. He sank back on the seat. Those shots were intended for him!

But who knew he was on the train!?

Only Melissa.

Worthy checked in the hotel, saying he was going west in the morning. He was given a room on the fourth floor, and he went up to bed at once.

But he could not sleep. He turned and twisted, but sleep would not come. His mind was wide awake. Trying to read between the lines of his sister's brief telegram, he feared that whoever had killed his father might want to finish the job— might want to kill them all—all the Bancrofts!

Who could such a monster be? Worthy thought back over the names he'd heard his father mention, but there were so many! W.R. Bancroft had been in money and politics in San Francisco for many years, for as many years as Worthy could remember. How could one know where to start?

Then Worthy remembered something his father had been fond of saying: "There are no accidents in life."

Had that shooting on the way to the hotel been deliberate? Had someone put out the word that Worthington Bancroft was to die? And, to carry his reasoning a step further, were his mother and sister also slated to die?

Worthy did not even consider why; he just knew he must get to San Francisco as soon as possible!

In the morning, an hour before the train was to leave, he had a solid breakfast, then bought a Colt revolver and a box of ammunition at the gun shop. He felt it would be a very good idea to be prepared.

He was able to obtain a berth in a hotel Pullman car on the Chicago and North Western Railway, touted as the shortest route between Chicago and Omaha.

Just before boarding the train, he wired Melissa that he was on his way, just leaving Chicago. He begged her to take every precaution, telling her that he thought she might be in danger.

In Omaha, he received an answer to his telegram. His sister *was* taking every precaution. She assured him that she had told no one except trusted friends that he was coming by train.

But someone knew.

As Worthy was returning to his room from the dining car on the first night out of Omaha, he was confronted by two toughs. They said nothing at all but sprang at him as he passed from one car to the next. His reactions were automatic. Young and strong, Worthy had been a championship boxer in college. The two toughs were at a slight disadvantage in the narrow car, since both could not reach Worthy at the same time, as hard as they tried.

An open-handed straight-arm to the chin of the first man stunned him. Worthy yelled loudly as he jumped at the second tough, startling him. Then Worthy kicked out at the man's knee and swung an elbow at the same time. The man was hurt, but he swore and jerked a knife from under his coat. The second man forced open the outside door.

"Push him out!"

Worthy could hear the loud clacking of the wheels on the rails and felt the sudden inrush of cold night air. The two toughs wanted to toss him off the train! He put his back to the wall and lifted both feet, smashing them into each other. The man wielding the knife doubled up, dropped the weapon and stumbled forward. Worthy yelled again and charged. He shouldered the tough, who caromed off his surprised partner and fell into the void.

The other was astonished, looking after his friend, mouth open. Worthy kicked the knife through the open door and off the train as the stunned man recovered, flailed with both fists, and screamed at him, "You lousy sonofabitch!"

Warding off the blows expertly, Worthy kicked again at the man's chin—and connected. The tough staggered back, and Worthy hit him twice more as he fell to sprawl on the dusty floor, out cold.

Worthy's first thought was to toss the man after his partner, but he decided against it. Reluctantly, he trussed up the tough using the man's own belt and neckerchief. Then he called for the conductor and closed the open door.

When the conductor arrived and listened to Worthy's story, he had two porters carry the unconscious man to an empty compartment to be imprisoned until the police at the next stop could take him in hand.

The conductor locked the compartment from the outside, saying there had been several attempts at robbery on his train recently, and he was very sorry it had happened to Worthy.

Worthy explained that he had thrown the prisoner's partner off the train, and the conductor might want to tell the police about where they should look for him. He did not tell the conductor the attack had been something other than a simple robbery attempt.

He was positive now that his sister was correct. Someone had wired to Chicago and had hired those toughs to get rid of him before he could get home. The Bancroft family was in terrible danger.

He must wire Melissa not to meet him when he arrived in San Francisco. It wasn't safe.

The following morning, the conductor came to Worthy's berth. "I'm afraid I have bad news, Mr. Bancroft."

"Oh? What is it?"

"The man you captured yesterday has escaped. Somehow he managed to break the door lock and has jumped off the train. We made a thorough search, and he is nowhere to be found. I am very sorry."

"Damn!"

"He may have had a tool on his person that we missed when we searched him. I really don't know what to say."

"Yes, well, it's too bad, but it's not your fault."

41

But at least both men were off the train. Worthy reflected that this ought to mean he would have no further trouble. Not until he reached San Francisco.

Ki found Silas Dent's office in the Harding Building on Cargill Street. Dent occupied one entire floor, and when Ki sent his name in, Silas came to the floor of his inner office and shook hands with Ki.

"Haven't seen you in a coon's age! Come in, come on in. Where's Jessica?" he asked, looking past Ki.

"She'll see you soon."

"Good, good." Dent was a lanky man with a narrow hawk-nosed face. He pointed to a chair and closed the door. "Now, what brings you two to San Francisco?"

"Trouble," Ki said. "You know about the Worthington Bancroft accident?"

"Yes. Too bad about W.R. and his wife. From what I hear, she might as well be dead." Dent sat behind his desk. "Are you and Jessie interested in that?"

"Melissa Bancroft says it was murder."

"I see." Dent found a cigar, offered one to Ki, and lighted up. "There sure was a big funeral, and the newspapers were full of it. But, I gotta say, the papers didn't mention murder, you know."

"Yes, I know. Well, Jessie went to school with Melissa Bancroft, and the two are very good friends. Naturally, we'll look into it for her. Besides, as you can imagine, Jessie finds this case a little too close to her own situation not to investigate. You know how hard she took her own father's murder."

"Right. How can I help?"

"Your knowledge of San Francisco politicians will be invaluable. Did you know Worthington Bancroft or any of his family personally?"

"Certainly. W.R. was a fine man. You want to know his enemies and his friends? Who can be trusted, who can't, who might have wanted him out of the way and so on?"

"Exactly."

"Then let me make some notes. Where are you staying? Where can I reach you?"

"Jessie and I are here separately. She's taken rooms at the Palace Hotel but will be moving in with Melissa. I haven't gotten a room yet. Where would you suggest?"

"The Nugget," Silas said at once. "It's a smallish hotel on Stockton Street, but there's several ways in and out. It would be hard for someone to watch them all. The manager-owner is an old friend of mine, too. His name is George Daley. Tell him you know me, and he'll do good by you."

"Fine. I will."

"I want to see Jessie soon—"

Ki rose and headed for the door. "I'll tell her. I know she wants to see you, too."

Chapter 7

A few hours before the train would reach San Francisco, Worthy received another wire from his sister telling him that his "old flame" Jessica Starbuck would meet him at the station because their mother was too ill for Melissa to leave her alone. The wire also joked that it had been such a long time since he and Jessie had seen each other that she was going to wear a red bow in her hair so he would recognize her. It was signed with love from Melissa and Jessica.

Worthy knew exactly what was happening. He remembered Jessica dimly, his sister's friend from Texas, a luscious-looking female who left a trail of brokenhearted males behind her wherever she went. He would be delighted to see that particular green-eyed beauty again. And he was pleased that he was to pretend to be her beau.

But when the train finally rattled in to the drafty San Francisco station, Worthy was met by two policemen. While the older uniformed officer hung back in deference, the younger one in plainclothes showed Worthy a badge and introduced himself as Inspector Jenkins. "Will you come with us, Mr. Bancroft." It was not a question.

The police positioned themselves one on either side of Worthy, and as they started out, Jessica ran up and threw her arms around him. "Worthy! I'm so glad I found you! Oh, I missed you so much!" She planted a kiss on his smiling lips.

As he held her, he looked at her appraisingly. "Hello, my dearest. You'll never know just how much I've missed you. We have a lot of catching up to do." He kissed her hard, and she squirmed in his grasp.

Inspector Jenkins said, "Really, you two, we've no time for this—"

Jessica clung to Worthy. "No time?! But I haven't seen him in years!" She looked at him in surprise. "Worthy, who are these men, and why were you heading off with them? Didn't you get our wire?"

"Yes, Jessie, my love, I did. But these gentlemen are the police."

She batted her thick lashes at Jenkins. "Police! Oh, isn't that so exciting! What a fascinating man you must be! Just imagine—the police!" She fluttered her lace fan and smiled at the inspector.

Jenkins took a long breath. "My dear young lady, this man is in police custody. I must ask you to run along—"

Worthy said, "Just a minute! Are you arresting me?"

"No, no . . . we only want to ask you some questions, that's all."

"Then ask them."

"Oh, yes. Ask them, sir," Jessica said, smiling sweetly at Jenkins as she leaned forward so he could catch the subtle scent of her perfume and perhaps look down the neck of her low-cut gown.

Jenkins became slightly flustered. "We'll ask our questions . . . at the station. Now, if you'll—"

"Oh, how fun! I *must* see what a police station looks like! Won't that be exciting, Worthy! Will you show me around, sir? Oh, please?"

Jenkins caved in. "All right, come along." He gave the other policemen a look that said: *She's harmless*. Then he appeared to change his mind. "We won't bother with the station house this time," he said. "Riley, I think we'll use one of the rooms here at the depot." He cleared his throat and took on a businesslike demeanor. "Sergeant, arrange it with the station master right away."

Riley nodded and walked away. He was back in a few

moments, crooking his finger. They followed him into a small office room, and he closed the door.

"Sit down, please—both of you," Jenkins said quietly. He stood before them as Jessica held Worthy's hand. "I'm very sorry about your father's death, Mr. Bancroft. Is there anything you can tell us that will help our investigation?"

"My sister says you think Carlos Ortega had something to do with my mother's injury and my father's murder, which is nonsense, of course."

Jenkins stiffened. "Your sister is overwrought, Mr. Bancroft. We are practically certain the *accident* was caused by Ortega's negligence. It was definitely not murder."

"If you believe that," Worthy said, "then I have nothing further to say to you."

"The inquest has held that the death of your father and the injuries to your mother were caused by the driver's negligence," Jenkins stated in a flat voice. "We have a warrant for Ortega's arrest."

Worthy and Jessica rose. She clung to his arm.

Jenkins said sharply, "We believe your sister is hiding Ortega."

Worthy shrugged. "Carlos is not a murderer." He showed Jessica to the door. Turning back, he said, "If Melissa is hiding him, she is using good sense." He opened the door, and the two went out.

They hurried through the train station and found a cab on a side street. Piling in his luggage, he said, "God! They actually think Carlos did it! That is incredible! They must be insane or corrupt." He helped Jessica in and sat beside her.

"Ortega couldn't have been paid to do it?"

He shook his head. "Under no circumstances. Any of us would trust Carlos with our lives." He looked at her. "You certainly flustered the inspector."

"I tried to." She smiled for a moment. "My friend and traveling companion, Ki, has gone to see an old friend of my father's, Silas Dent. Do you know him?"

"I believe I've heard the name."

"He knows everyone. I feel you and Melissa are in great danger. You two must stay in the house and leave only with Ki or me. Did you have any trouble on the train?"

Worthy told her of the incidents in Chicago and outside Omaha, and she sighed and shook her head. "They *are* after you. Whoever *they* are. Have you any ideas whatsoever about who's behind all this?"

"I'm afraid not."

"Why was your father killed?"

"That's the crucial question. Why? I haven't been gone that long, but I don't have any idea why."

Jessica said, "If we find out the answer, we'll probably know the killer. Melissa thinks it was Josiah Kelton. Do you know him?"

Worthy shook his head. "Not personally. I've met him once or twice is all. I know what he looks like. He might not remember me."

"If Melissa is right, he knows more about you than you would think. But why he would want to tear down the Bancroft empire is a mystery."

Worthy looked at her. She was probably right. He knew very little about Kelton, but the gossip said the saloon owner was a man to be feared.

It was astonishing how Jessica had changed, Worthy marveled to himself, from the meeting with the two policemen when she seemed to be such a scatterbrained ball of fluff. Now, she was a level-headed woman who was all business yet still breathtakingly beautiful.

He glanced at the dark street now and then, but it was hard to tear his eyes away from her. So many of the women he met were really scatterbrains because women were not allowed to have opinions of their own in many cases. Jessica was a refreshing change who stimulated both his mind and his body. There would be many possibilities pretending to be her beau.

And when he took her hand to tell her how thankful he was that she and Ki were helping him, she didn't pull away. How very refreshing—and inviting.

Chapter 8

Melissa was overjoyed to see her brother. When Garfield opened the door, she pulled Worthy into the house and fell into his arms. She was crying softly as she embraced him and clung tightly to him, and Jessica had to daub her eyes with a lace handkerchief.

Worthy said gently, "I'm here—and in one piece! What's all the fuss?"

"It's just that I'm so relieved to finally see you. Oh, Worthy!"

"Everything is fine, now, Missy. I'm here." He headed toward the staircase. "I must see Mother. Is she awake?"

Melissa's face dropped. "It doesn't really matter. Do go on up. Jessie and I will be in the sitting room."

Garfield brought Worthy's bags in while Melissa and Jessica went into the small sitting room. Melissa poured coffee for them, and Jessie related the events at the station while they waited for Worthy.

As soon as he joined them, his eyes moist and his voice husky, Worthy said, "I want to speak with Carlos as soon as it can be arranged."

Melissa shook her head. "We don't know where he is. Garfield will meet him in a couple of days."

"You know the police want to arrest him for negligence. They blame him for our parents' tragedy!"

48

"Yes. And they're watching the house." Melissa sighed. "Everything has changed all of a sudden! It's as if we are all criminals!"

Jessica sipped her coffee and nodded.

Worthy said, "On the night of the accident, W.R. and Mother had gone to the Kelton house for dinner. Is that right?"

"Yes," Melissa said.

"Whatever made them do that? Why would W.R. drag Mother to such a place?"

Melissa shook her head. "Father thought he should attend the party. I got the impression he and Kelton were having problems—very serious problems."

Jessica asked, "Who exactly is this Josiah Kelton?"

Worthy said, "He's the owner of the Gold Dust Saloon, which has a big gambling house upstairs. He's very rich, but no one on Nob Hill will accept him. His reputation is not of the best, as you can well imagine. Missy, why would Father—"

"I honestly don't know. But I've been going through Father's effects. Evidently he and Kelton had been having secret dealings for a long, long time."

Jessica said, "Kelton's a gambler and a gang leader?"

Melissa nodded.

Worthy asked, "What kind of dealings could W.R. have with the likes of Josiah Kelton?"

Melissa shook her head. "I couldn't tell from Father's papers. You know how circumspect Father was; he made notes for his eyes only." She paused. "And there's one other thing . . ."

"What?"

"Father had also been meeting with someone in secret, and I'm quite certain it was someone with a most questionable background . . . and not Kelton."

Worthy groaned. "This gets worse and worse."

Melissa said, "I think it was someone Father knew years before. Both Carlos and Garfield mentioned him."

"A mystery man?"

"Yes, and he walks with a limp." Melissa took a deep breath. "We both know that Father had a rather exciting life,

49

to put it mildly, before he settled down. Mother used to re-count such thrilling tales. I suspect this mystery man was part of that."

"You mean, from his college days or his years as a pros-pector in the gold or silver fields?"

Melissa shrugged. "I don't know." She smiled at Jessie. "That's something we'll have to find out, won't we?"

Jessica nodded and winked.

Worthy said, "I wonder if this mystery man had anything to do with Father's death."

Melissa put down her cup. "We don't know enough to even guess at this point."

Worthy got up and went to the window. "Mother was asleep when I went up just now." He cleared his throat. "I'd like to speak with her."

Melissa swallowed hard. "She'll probably sleep through until morning. You can look in on her then."

Jessie said, "She's so pale and fragile. Is she any better now than she was right after the accident? Has there been any improvement?"

Melissa brightened. "Yes, a bit. Dr. Witherspoon is quite encouraged. Her memory is slowly returning. But you know how Father was; he probably told her absolutely nothing of his dealings. I doubt if Mother will be of any help even when her memory is fully recovered."

Zack and Grady clumped up the stairs to Kelton's office, each one wanting the other to go in first. Kelton's famous temper was certain to be turned against them. Grady rapped hesi-tantly, and they both unwillingly piled into the room at Kel-ton's growl.

Kelton looked them over. They were obviously a couple of prize losers. He snarled, "Now what?"

"The cops met Bancroft when he got off the train, boss. We didn't have no chance at all to get near him. Honest."

They were both surprised when their employer nodded. He had expected that. "All right. How many you got watching the Bancroft house?"

"Three, boss, around the clock."

"Yeh? Well, what about Ortega?"

Grady shrugged. "He ain't turned up yet. If he comes to the house, we'll grab 'im. It's a big town."

Kelton roared, "I know it's a big goddamn town!" He took a deep breath. "A'right. Go see you watch the house. That's our best chance."

The two gunmen hurried out.

Kelton lit a cigar, got up, and paced to the window. The damn Bancroft kid had a charmed life, apparently. He had eluded the men sent against him on the train and arrived in San Francisco without a scratch.

Well, when you hire toughs at long distance, you can't expect the best, he mused. But it had been worth trying anyway. Worthy was here in The City now, and it should not be all that difficult to put a hole in him somewhere fatal.

Whether or not Zack and Grady were capable of pulling it off was another matter. Young Bancroft had proved himself very able on the train. This was something to think about.

Ki came into the house at midnight, eluding the police. There were three men watching the house, he told them. Two seemed half-asleep.

He had met with Silas Dent, and the old friend of Alex Starbuck had agreed to help them in every way he could. He was preparing a list of all of W.R.'s friends and enemies, and he had suggested a good hotel for their purposes that was not too far from Nob Hill.

As they discussed the case, both Ki and Jessie expressed extreme interest in Josiah Kelton and in the old man with the limp—the mystery man.

Ki looked from Worthy to Melissa. "You have no idea who he is?"

"None at all," Melissa said. "Nor what he wanted here with my father."

Ki said, "Why don't we ask the servants if they have seen him. We just might learn something. Surely one of them has seen him."

Melissa rose. "I'll call Garfield." She pulled the bell cord,

51

and when Garfield appeared, she asked him about the man with the limp.

The butler had indeed seen the man—several times. "Mr. Bancroft let him into the house, Miss Melissa."

"What!? My father did?"

"Yes, Miss Melissa. Such a ragged, dirty old man he was. He was brought in the back door."

Jessica asked, "Can you tell us what he looked like?"

"Yus, mum. He wore an old cloak, black or dark blue. It was too filthy to tell. The brim of his dark hat was turned down so I was unable to see his face. But he had long scraggly gray hair, and he walked with a decided limp."

"But you don't know who he was? Did Mr. Bancroft call him by name?"

"No, mum. Not so's I could hear."

The other servants were called in one by one.

Mrs. Oglethorpe had not seen the old man with the limp at all. Juanita had, and her description was very close to Garfield's. Juanita's impression was that the old man was a beggar; she had not seen him enter the house. None of the maids had seen the man. The stableboys were not sure and were too intimidated by everyone to answer one way or the other.

"A mystery man with a game leg," Ki commented. "But obviously someone who knew your father."

Melissa sighed. "Perhaps someone down on his luck that Father helped. He was always giving financial assistance to the less fortunate."

Both Ki and Jessie felt it was imperative that they talk with Carlos. They instructed Garfield to go to the old market the following morning to meet him. He would arrange a meeting place with Jessie and Worthy.

Ki left then, well into the early hours of the morning, and returned to the Nugget Hotel. Jessie, in her disguise as a scatterbrained-blonde friend of Melissa's and old girlfriend of Worthy's, stayed behind. All business while not in public, Jessie checked every window and door, making certain the house was locked up tightly for the night, including the basement windows.

• • •

In the morning, Garfield was given another envelope containing money for Carlos, and he set out for the old market with his usual shopping bag and list. He met Carlos in one of the back stalls, did his buying, and returned to the mansion as quickly as possible.

Carlos was well, he reported. "He was not hit by a bullet at all." He told this to Juanita, who was greatly relieved. To Melissa and the others, he said, "Carlos will meet you by the lighthouse just north and east of Seal Rocks. He said he would be up inside the lighthouse, watching to see if you had been followed."

"There's a picnic grounds there," said Melissa. "The grounds were especially leveled and cleared of underbrush so women could take their children there. Carlos must have chosen that site because there are half a dozen paths in and out, and he can observe them all from above."

"Good," Ki said. "What time?"

"Just at sunset. He will show himself when it becomes dark. He felt it would be safer that way."

"Good work," Ki said, slapping the butler's shoulder. "You are the best spy we know."

It was decided that Worthy and Jessica would take a picnic basket to the grounds near the lighthouse and pose as lovers. The basket would give them an excuse to be in the park for hours. It was agreed that Melissa would stay home.

The following afternoon, Worthy had one of the stableboys drop Jessie and him off at the park. It was a pleasant place of grass and windswept trees high atop a promontory at the foot of the lighthouse. Just at the entrance to the bay, the sweeping panorama of sea crashing on rocks below and Point Reyes far across the inlet was breathtaking. Children played ball on the grass and whooped and yelled as their mothers and nannies watched over them protectively.

Jessie spread a blanket on the grass; Worthy placed the picnic basket on it; and they sat waiting for the sun to set and Carlos to appear.

Worthy was wearing jeans and a blue shirt under a loose coat. Ki had fitted him with a shoulder holster and a pistol.

Worthy had never worn such a holster before, but he knew how to use the pistol. "I was a crack shot at Harvard."

Jessica was wearing a long pink dress, matching bonnet, and a light cape. She wore jeans underneath her dress and carried a pistol in her purse.

Worthy was fascinated with the blonde beauty. Did she really have the reputation of a woman who was as fast with a gun as she was with a smile? Women were not supposed to be gunslingers, at least not in Worthy's world.

Jessie put out cold chicken and a bottle of wine, and they talked about horses and sailing. She fed him bits of chicken, and he poured her more wine. They laughed and held hands, and Worthy leaned over to brush her cheek with his lips.

"Do you think we were followed here?" he asked, kissing her cheek again.

"Yes, we were." She pulled away and giggled coyly.

He looked at her in astonishment. Taking her in his arms, he smelled the fragrance of her soft honey-blonde hair and asked, "You saw someone follow us?"

"Yes." Again she pulled away, patted him playfully on his cheek and let him pull her close again. "He was sitting right over there half an hour ago. He's gone now. I have a feeling he's waiting for the park to clear out. Too many people . . . too many witnesses."

Worthy looked around, wide eyed.

Jessie touched his arm and pushed him down onto the blanket. "Don't be so obvious, dear." She rolled onto her back and let him prop himself above her.

Under normal circumstances, Worthy would have made love to her, but all he could think of was the man following them. His nose rubbed her chin as he said, "But are you saying someone wants to do something to us?"

She sat up quickly, fussing with her hair. "I don't know. But it's possible." She put things back in the basket. "Maybe Carlos noticed the man, too. Why don't we take a nice little walk along the cliff?"

"All right." Worthy got up slowly, pressing his arm against the comforting bulk of the revolver inside his coat.

They left the blanket and the basket and strolled toward the lighthouse, appearing to be completely wrapped up in each other. If Carlos had seen the man who followed her, Jessie thought, he might not show himself.

The park had cleared somewhat, young children being bundled up and led to waiting carriages. A few couples were still sitting here and there on the grass or strolling along the cliff. Jessie took Worthy's arm as if they too were young lovers. The man she had seen was skinny, with a look of a pickpocket or worse. She had not detected any signal that he might have made to confederates, but they might easily be nearby, waiting to pounce on Carlos.

She said in a low voice to Worthy, "I hope Carlos stays away from here."

"Yes, so do I." He took her in his arms and kissed her slowly.

This time she did not pull away. Her body pressed firmly against his, and Worthy wished the circumstances for their picnic could have been different. He was enjoying this beauty's company far too much.

The sun had slipped down into the ocean, and a fog was rolling in off the water. A very welcome sight, Jessica remarked to Worthy. They strolled past the lighthouse without seeing Carlos. Moving away from the cliff, they entered the trees. A few other couples were also taking the air, talking and holding hands. Guitar music came wafting from behind a hedge.

It was getting dark fast now. The sun had dipped into the ocean and disappeared from view. Jessie felt a twinge of concern. If they were indeed being followed by the man she had seen and his unseen accomplices, then it must be Worthy they were after, as well as Carlos.

And if Carlos had spotted these men, he would stay under cover, avoiding capture. She must then get Worthy out of any possible trap she might have led him into.

Opening her purse as if to powder her nose, she brought out her metal mirror and primped for a moment. As she returned the mirror, she slid her hand inside and curled her fingers around the butt of her pistol. She and Worthy had stayed much too long in the park, hoping for Carlos to appear.

If any harm came to Worthy while he was with her, how could she ever face Melissa!

Was that her imagination, or was that a flitting figure off to the right in the trees?

She pressed Worthy's arm, and they turned, moving toward the left. She said quietly, "You must join any group of people we come across, blend in, and—"

"What about you?" He looked at her in surprise.

"They're after you, not me. You must get out of this place as soon as possible. Please!"

"But—"

She squeezed his arm and kissed his cheek warmly. "Don't argue with me. I know what I'm talking about. As I said, they don't want me."

Worthy turned his head to remonstrate with her, and she suddenly pushed him to one side. A man had appeared in front of them with a leveled pistol. The gunman ignored her, aiming point-blank at Worthy. There was only a second. Jessica tilted her handbag up and fired through the bottom of it. The gunman's shot tore into the ground at Worthy's feet as the man slumped, dropping his pistol.

Worthy swore in surprise, staring at Jessica. She knelt by the would-be assassin and felt for a pulse. There was none. She shook her head, gathered up his pistol, and motioned to Worthy. "Go that way."

He did as she told him. This beautiful young woman was a tigress!

The fog was setting in, thick and swirling, shortening the distances. And it suddenly seemed as if everyone in the park had left. They were alone. Jessica thought she heard a shout behind them, perhaps someone had found the body. If it was the gunman's friends, this would probably enrage them.

Worthy said in a whisper, "I don't recognize any of this. I think we've wandered out of the park."

Jessie gripped his arm. "Shhh! Wait." She cocked her head, putting her extraordinary senses to the test, listening. She could hear the distant sound of the surf crashing against the rocks below the cliff, only a murmur. Seagulls cried overhead. There was no wind, and the fog smelled salty and close. There was no sound at all from the city nearby.

Jessica suddenly realized she was not sure of directions. In the dense fog, she had lost her bearings.

Off to the right there was a movement, and in a moment, a shot was fired. It cracked by only yards away as the couple ducked and ran. Worthy halted, wanting to turn and fight his assailant, but Jessica pushed him, rasping, "Go, for God's sake, don't stop!"

The pursuers had spotted them. Now they would close in for the kill if there were enough of them.

The couple dashed through the trees and came to a ditch. Jessica jumped down, calling softly, "Come on." Holding up her skirts and tucking them under her belt, she ran along the ditch, aware that they were moving slightly uphill. Doubtless it was a storm runoff, and they were heading away from the ocean, just the way she wanted to go.

In a few minutes she halted, listening again.

Worthy said, "I think we've lost 'em."

"Maybe."

Was that an alien sound out there? Jessie motioned Worthy down. As they ducked under overhanging brush, they could hear a horseman approaching. The rider came to within a few yards of them and halted. Jessie took a firm grip on Worthy's arm to keep him from jumping up and exchanging shots with the enemy. She knew she was right when she looked into Worthy's face. His eyes flashed with intensity as his body strained against her grip.

Then the rider moved on, walking the horse. Jessica stood up warily. She could just barely see the back of the man's head as he rode on and disappeared in the fog.

Jessica and Worthy climbed out of the ditch and hurried in the direction from which the rider had come. That seemed to be the most natural route to take.

In a moment, another rider loomed up. Seeing the couple, the gunman pulled a pistol and fired. In the same instant, Jessie got a shot off. The rider's bullet picked at Worthy's sleeve as the gunman toppled from his saddle. Jessica fired again before he hit the ground.

Worthy's pistol was now in his hand, ready for business.

But he had barely pulled back the hammer in the time it took Jessica to fire twice! God! What a tigress! He watched her examine the fallen foe and shake her head again.

This one was dead, too. Worthy took a long breath. The young blonde was a dead shot! Her green eyes hooded, she beckoned him and ran on, tucking the hem of her skirts back under her belt as she went.

In minutes, they came to a road and turned onto it. The fog, like a low cloud, seemed to swallow them. It was turning quite chilly, and they both shivered as they trotted along. The road led them to a street where there were houses—civilization. Just ahead, Worthy could see a row of storefront buildings. They had made it! Thanks to Jessica's heightened senses and amazing shooting.

Worthy looked at Jessica. She had pulled her skirts out of her belt and let them drop. Both her pistol and the one she had picked up were in her frilly handbag. As she walked sedately along, she appeared to be merely a lovely young woman who had nary a worry or a care, who would never know what in the world to do if menaced by some ugly gunman bent on killing her.

Worthy sighed inwardly. He wouldn't want to be that gunman!

Chapter 9

Grady, watching the Bancroft mansion on the afternoon shift, was surprised to see young Bancroft driven away with a blonde woman beside him. Was it the same blonde floozie who had met him at the train? It looked like it.

Grady sent a message to Zack and followed with three others. Maybe they would get a chance to center the kid.

Young Bancroft went right to the old lighthouse park and got out of the carriage with the blonde on one arm and a picnic basket on the other. The carriage drove away.

Grady put his men around the park with orders to shoot to kill the kid if they got a chance to get him alone. Forget the girl, center the kid. There was a bonus in it for the man that plugged him.

It was annoying as hell when the fog started rolling in and the sun went down. But it was good that the park was clearing out.

When the couple got up and strolled along the cliff, Grady tried to follow, but he had to stay a good distance behind or they would spot him.

But he ran when he heard the shot.

He swore when he came to the body. That sonofabitch Worthy Bancroft had shot Sims! Grady could hardly believe it, but Sims was dead as a fish.

Later on, Penry had gotten unlucky, too. Two slugs had put

an end to him! Jesus! Kelton hadn't told them that young Bancroft was so handy with a gun!

Bancroft and the blonde floozie had gotten clean away!

As Grady had expected, Kelton swore something fierce when he reported to him. A good chance had gone glimmering.

"The damn kid killed two fast men, boss! You didn't tell us—"

"How would I know?" Kelton yelled. "Do I play patty-cake with him! Get the hell outa here!"

When Jessie and Worthy arrived back to civilization, they hailed a cab and drove straight to the Bancroft mansion. Jessie knew there was nothing to fear from killers with police surrounding the house, waiting to pounce on Carlos Ortega. The gunmen would not be brazen enough to shoot Worthy in sight of police, since not all could be on the pad.

Melissa rushed to the door to greet Jessica and Worthy. She had not expected them to be so late in returning from their tryst with Carlos. "Are you all right? What did Carlos say? Were you followed? What took you so long?" Questions came tumbling out, one after another. Jessica and Worthy had no chance to reply.

Jessica laughed as Worthy put a brotherly arm around his sister and gave her a loving squeeze. "Missy," Jessie said, "we're here, aren't we? You can see we're just fine."

"Yes, but you took so long."

Worthy said, "There was an ambush. Some men tried to gun us down. Jessie was just brilliant—"

Melissa blanched and gasped audibly, her hands covering her mouth as she looked from Worthy to Jessie.

Smiling warmly, Jessie said, "We are fine, Missy. Really we are. You know I would never have let anything happen to Worthy."

"Yes, but . . ."

Jessica understood. Having lost her father—and for all intents and purposes, her mother, too—the idea of losing her brother was just too horrible for Melissa to imagine. Jessie tried to minimize the gunplay at the lighthouse, telling her how Carlos must have spotted the men following them and never showed up. "It was a lovely day for a picnic. We'll meet with Carlos another day."

But Worthy was ebullient and wouldn't be stopped. "Oh, Missy, you should have seen her! What a shot! What a woman!" The admiration went far beyond mere appreciation.

Jessie said to them both, "It's late and we need our sleep. Let's all get some rest. We have much to do, and time is growing short. Time is on the side of the killer, and it has become obvious that someone wants the entire Bancroft family out of the way." She smiled brightly, her huge green eyes lingering on Worthy imperceptibly. "Enough morbid talk. Let's get to bed!"

Melissa, picking up on Jessie's playful attitude, giggled lightly and nodded. "To bed."

Worthy watched as Jessie padded from one room to the next, checking all the doors and windows. *What a tigress*! he thought as she prowled the entire premises. There was something quite stimulating about her strength. Desire was heating his body and flexing his muscles. He nodded to her as she approached, indicating she should go up first. He waited until she was well up the stairs before he extinguished the sitting room lamp and followed by the glow of his candle.

Stopping at his sister's room, he knocked. "Night, Missy." He heard a muffled "Night! Love you." from within. At Jessie's door, he paused and knocked. As he was about to speak, the door swung open, revealing a semiclad beauty whose long blonde tresses fell softly across her voluptuous bosom. His mouth opened, but words refused to come.

Taking his hand in hers, Jessica led him into her room and shut the door behind him. Silently, she took the candle from him and placed it on the bureau, never taking her eyes from his. He reached out, free hand encircling her soft white neck, and pulled her to him. She was in his arms, warm, supple, yielding. His lips sought hers hungrily, and his tongue brushed the width of her smile. He felt her body quiver as she kissed him in return. His captive manhood was throbbing for release.

Worthy's hand slipped under her negligee as he gently stroked her smooth flesh, cupping her firm buttocks and pulling her body to him. Her lashes fluttered and a small sigh escaped her lips as she clung to him, her arms around his shoulders. Her negligee fell to the floor revealing large pink nipples on two perfect breasts. Before he could reach for them, he sensed her fingers moving down his back, down his trousers, toward the front. She was undoing the buckle of his belt. It was his turn to sigh and moan. Her fingers fumbled with the front of his trousers, and he could stand no more.

Worthy scooped her up in his arms and carried her to the bed, kissing her long and hard. He laid her down on the waiting sheets and pulled off his boots, stepping out of his unbuttoned trousers. In a moment, he stood before her, naked and full of desire, his manhood saluting her beauty.

Jessie reached up and took his erection in her soft hand, caressing the sensitive head gently with her thumb. His knees went weak and he fell forward. She held on to his pulsing staff as he leaned to her breasts and took one into his mouth. His tongue tantalizing the nipple to total erection as he fondled the other.

Then his hand sought her moistness, dipping down into her furry cleft, probing her silky lower lips until he found her nob of pleasure. As he stroked it, she groaned and pushed her pelvis toward him. Her body was pleading with his, and he wanted her—his tigress.

Straddling her rounded thighs, he lowered himself slowly until he staff dipped into her wetness. She moaned loudly, hissing, "Yes-s-s!" His pelvis met hers and she pushed toward him, enveloping his shaft to the hilt. Grinding herself against him, she moved her hips round and round, twisting and gyrating with passion.

As she called his name, a fire swept through him and he plunged deeper and deeper into her silky inner regions. Her nails dug into his naked back as she writhed and clamped his body to her with her legs. They rolled over until she was on top of him, and he took both her breasts in his hands, nipping one nipple and then the other as she thrust herself harder and harder against him.

He pulled her down onto him so her rigid nipples poked into his chest, and she groaned and rolled over onto her back again, pulling him on top of her. Suddenly her eyes clamped shut and she arched her spine, panting and gasping, then held her breath as a delicious moan started deep from within and shuddered through her entire body. As her hot inner flesh tightened and spasmed around his shaft, he thrust faster and deeper until he felt a sudden release and flooded her with his appreciation.

Worthy stayed linked with Jessie, holding her nakedness to him. His face buried in her neck, he murmured, "My tigress, my kitten!" and kissed the tip of her nose affectionately. When their bodies parted, Jessie nestled herself in Worthy's arm, kissed his shoulder softly, and fell asleep. Worthy lay there, trying to remember the excitement of the day, but sleep cut off his happy thoughts.

Jessica, in a flouncy green Paris creation that matched her eyes, left the Bancroft mansion alone in a carriage. Worthy and Melissa would stay inside. The shots yesterday had been for Worthy; Kelton, if it indeed were Kelton who had sent the assassins, obviously played for keeps.

The police who watched the house looking for Carlos Ortega, did not follow her. Neither did Kelton's men. She was only a foolish, empty-headed young woman.

Jessie left the carriage in the city and strolled from one fancy store to the next, browsing, talking to clerks, continuing her role as a light-headed blonde nothing, just in case she was being watched.

She went to the Palace Hotel for a late lunch, fending off too-eager males who wished to lay themselves at her feet. She laughed to herself, playing this role was amusing. It had been a long time since she'd done such foolish things. She was glad Ki was nowhere near to smile at her feminine antics. She knew her bobbing breasts attracted attention and her blank smile enticed men. She was all too aware of their hungry stares.

Lunch over, she slipped away from her admirers, into a hotel stairwell and down several halls to her private suite. She changed into jeans, blouse, and boots, rearranged her hair completely, and strapped on a revolver under her cloak.

63

She ducked out of the hotel by a side door and hailed a hack. She had herself driven at once to the Nugget Hotel, where she met Ki. Then she and Ki went to Silas Dent's office.

Silas was delighted to see Jessica again after such a long time, hugging her and taking her arm to go into his inner office. "My dear, you look ravishing, even in that get-up!"

"You always were such a flatterer, Silas."

"Never! I tell the absolute truth at all times."

Jessie laughed. It was good to be among old friends she could trust.

Silas sat behind his desk and motioned his guests to be seated. "Since Ki arrived, I've been making notes." He held up a sheaf of papers. "All this pertains to W.R. Bancroft. Would you like to hear the facts or read it yourself?"

"By all means, tell us," said Ki.

"Here goes, then." Silas cleared his throat and leaned back, making himself comfortable. "When W.R. got out of college in the East—he attended Harvard, in case you're interested—he came west and went into prospecting. From all I can learn, he was very successful, being an extremely smart man, you understand. He is reputed to have taken close to forty million dollars in silver and gold out of the Comstock in Nevada. This was in the eighteen fifties and sixties."

Jessie said, "He must have been a very busy man when he hit it rich, then."

"He was. And as success began coming his way, he sent for his childhood sweetheart, Penelope, whom he had married before heading west, and their two children."

She asked, "How long did Penelope have to wait before he finally sent for her?"

"Well, they were married while W.R. was still in college. A little over a year later, Worthy came along. Melissa was born a few years after Worthy."

Ki said, "Where was W.R. when he sent for his family?"

"Virginia City, Nevada."

Jessie confirmed, "So they lived in Virginia City?"

"Yes," said Silas. "And very poorly at first, they lived in tents, then shacks, while he cleaned out the claims. How Penelope put up with all that I suppose no one will ever know, but she did. I'm told she really loved him, and she has a little steel in her, too, you know. And, of course, there was W.R.'s promise of wealth and luxury, which he made good. But from all who know her, they say she'd have followed him without it."

Jessie asked, "He did all this prospecting alone?"

Silas smiled. "There is a rumor, or talk, or gossip—whatever you want to call it—that W.R. had partners before he became one of the 'Silver Kings' of the Comstock Lode along with Jim Fair, Jimmy Flood, Johnny Mackay, and Bill O'Brien."

"Well, who were his partners then?" asked Ki. "Were they the chaps you just mentioned?"

Silas shook his head. "I can't find that out. It's been a while, you know. Memories aren't dependable. Let me go on . . ." He coughed and cleared his throat again. "W.R. brought his family out of Nevada and settled in San Francisco. He built one of the most luxurious mansions on Nob Hill, rivaled only by those of Mark Hopkins and Leland Stanford. He put the children in private schools back East." He smiled at Jessica. "That's where you met Melissa and took her under your wing, your baby sister, so to speak."

Jessie smiled and nodded.

"W.R. turned his Harvard education to good use by becoming a stockbroker and a politician, as well as a philanthropist. He was a great man," Silas concluded.

"That's quite a history," Ki said appreciatively. "Bancroft came up the hard way."

"Nobody gave him anything," Silas said. "He earned it all, every penny he had." He put several of the pages aside and took up another piece of paper. "I've got something here on Josiah Kelton."

"Let's hear it," said Jessie.

"It's quite different from W.R.'s, I can tell you. His background is very sketchy, I suppose he wants it that way. He came from somewhere in the East and worked in the gold fields, but not for long. He returned to San Francisco with enough money to start a saloon and gambling houses. And business boomed." Silas smirked. "Of course, being the kind of man he is, he was never taken into high society and that rankled him. The man is a downright scoundrel. But he doesn't seem to realize it, or he somehow believes people do not see him as he really is."

Jessie said, "Melissa is sure he murdered her father."

Silas nodded. "Yes, and I tend to think that just might be true. He's that kind of man, and I know he and W.R. had many differences. But let me go on." He reached for a glass of some clear liquid, sipped slowly, and then continued. "Kelton has a woman friend, a mistress, called Carlotta Reardon, whom he refuses to marry. She acts as his hostess when he entertains at his Russian Hill home." Silas sniffed. "I have been there, and I can tell you, it's more like a bordello than a home. Naturally, Nob Hill people snicker at it behind his back, and most of them are his clients at the posh gambling salon he maintains over the saloon."

"Hmm. I'd like to go there," Jessica said. "Are women allowed?"

"Certainly. It's much different from the downstairs saloon or the regular gambling rooms. It's a very dressy place, quite elegant." Silas smiled. "You can fairly taste the refinement." He laughed.

"You've been there?" Jessie asked.

"Yes, indeed." Silas rattled the papers. "I must warn you, Kelton is feared by a great many people because it is generally felt that he is walking the ragged edge of the law. He will stop at nothing if it means money in his pocket."

"Are his tables honest?" Ki asked.

"Yes. If people thought they were not, no one would go there. I imagine Kelton gnashes his teeth every day because he doesn't dare fix them so they'll win more for him. He has a very quick temper; he's ruthless, and he'll seek revenge at the drop of a hat. And another thing, it is common knowledge that half of City Hall is on his payroll in one way or another. I've heard it said that he keeps blackmail files." Silas shrugged. "It may be true. Who knows?"

"What about W.R. and Kelton?" Jessie asked.

"That's interesting. It is well known that W.R. had been

visiting Kelton's gambling rooms and dropping quite a bundle almost weekly."

Ki was surprised. "He lost constantly?"

"Yes. And he had been looking worse and worse just before his death. As if something were getting him down, eating away at him. But his brokerage house was in excellent condition, and his bank balance rivaled the U.S. mint. Many of us decided he was the victim of emotional stress."

"Or some weighty secret," Jessica said.

Silas nodded. He passed a list across the desk. "Friends and enemies, not very many enemies, as you can see. W.R. was a good man, generous to a fault. He would help anyone who asked for assistance. However," he said, wagging a finger, "his dealings with corrupt politicians such as David Broderick were extremely puzzling. I have no answers for you about them."

"You've done wonderfully," said Jessie gratefully. "We've a much better picture of W.R. than before." She looked at the paper. "Hmmm, I see Josiah Kelton is number one on the enemies list."

"That's my feeling," Silas admitted. "I may be influenced by the fact that I wouldn't trust Josiah Kelton with a plugged Canadian penny. I personally think the man is a crook. Am I being too subtle?"

Jessica laughed. "Hardly." She rose, offering Silas her hand. "Thanks, old friend." She took his hand, gripped it firmly, and pulled him far enough across the desk to kiss him lightly on the cheek.

Silas beamed and then shook hands with Ki. "Now don't turn your back on Kelton at any time."

"We promise," Ki said soberly.

They split up the list to check out. Jessica felt she could meet some of W.R.'s friends if Melissa and Worthy would invite them to a dinner party in her honor at the Bancroft mansion. Ki felt he would like to visit Kelton's gambling rooms, where he might see some of W.R.'s enemies at close range, without any of them knowing who he was.

67

Melissa was agreeable to the dinner party and sat down immediately to plan the affair with Jessie.

Ki went to the Gold Dust Saloon and walked upstairs to the gambling rooms. He had no chance to enter the posh rooms, reserved for those in evening attire, but he was not interested in that aspect of Kelton's affairs, anyway.

Sipping a beer, Ki wandered from one table to another, watching the games in progress. It was a rather plain room, wood paneled and lighted by hanging gas lamps. Apparently, Ki thought, Kelton wanted nothing to distract his guests from losing money.

Two of the players attracted Ki's interest. They were apparently long-time guests, since they seemed to know everyone. Both were well-set-up men with flaming red hair. Very outgoing and vocal, tonight they were obviously winning for a change.

"It's about time!" one of them said to any and every one who would listen. "I been losin' at this stupid game for weeks now. But tonight Lady Luck is sittin' on my lap. I raise you a hunnert!" He shoved chips into the center of the table.

Ki asked a bystander, "Who are they?"

The man told him. "That's the O'Toole brothers, Patrick and Terrance. They struck it rich in the gold fields, then invested money in the largest wholesale butcher shop in this part of the country. They both love to gamble."

"So I see. Tell me, friend, what's the local opinion? Are these games honest?"

"They have to be, or nobody'd come in here."

Ki nodded. Exactly what Silas Dent had said. Most people hated horse thieves and card cheats. He watched the dealers closely and could detect nothing out of line.

And the O'Toole brothers won consistently. Lady Luck was indeed on their laps.

After a while, one of the players around the big felt-covered table got up with an excuse. "Deal me out a couple of rounds, boys," and went out.

Ki wandered after him, following the man down the hall. He listened at the door the man had gone into but could hear very little. Voices, no words, one of the voices was raised in anger. Then Ki had to scuttle away quickly as the door flew open and the man came out.

Ki gained an angle of the hall and watched the man return to the gambling room. In a moment, a man Ki took to be Josiah Kelton came out, puffing a cigar, and strode toward the gambling room to stand in the doorway for a few minutes.

The man Ki had followed probably reported that the O'Tooles were heavy winners, cleaning up. Kelton's reputation said that he hated to see large amounts of his money go out the door.

Kelton returned to his office, muttering to himself. He opened the door, then hesitated, seeming to change his mind, closed the door and hurried downstairs to the saloon. He was back in a short time with another man, a heavy, thick-shouldered tough with a battered face. They went into the office and slammed the door behind them.

Ki was sure. It was obvious, wasn't it, that Kelton was planning to get his money back from the much-too-lucky O'Toole brothers?

Shaking his head, Ki walked back into the gambling room. The brothers had amassed a small fortune and were cashing it in amid much joking and laughter. The bartenders were serving drinks to the house on the O'Tooles, who were preparing to leave.

Ki hurried downstairs. It was none of his affair if Kelton robbed the two gamblers, but he could not bring himself to allow it to happen as long as he knew about it. Melissa had said that Kelton was a crook; so had Silas Dent. And now Ki was positive it was true. He sat by the side of the street, head down, doing his best to look like a down-at-the-heels bum.

Immediately, the big heavy-shouldered thug came down the steps, shoving a pistol into the belt under his coat. He was followed by another equally disreputable-looking tough, and the two hurried around to the alley entrance at the side of the saloon. Neither paid any attention to the bum sitting there on the curb.

After a short interval, the O'Toole brothers came whooping down the stairs. They were laughing about their great streak of good fortune and how Kelton hated to see them take the money away, even though they had been leaving plenty of their own money there for months.

They walked around to the unlighted alleyway for their carriage.

Ki followed silently in the gloom. There were no lights in the street, and those from the Gold Dust Saloon did not reach halfway to the alley.

As he approached the mouth of the alley, Ki heard what he had expected. A heavy voice commanded, "Hands up, gents!"

The two brothers swore, and Ki saw them attack the would-be robbers. Instantly, there was a shot, then two more, a chorus of yells, and one of the O'Tooles was down. The other was pushed against the wall, his hands spread as the toughs snarled at him menacingly.

Ki stumbled into the alley, and the two thieves turned at once, revolvers pointing. Ki began to sing in an off-key, hic-coughing voice, still stumbling closer.

"It's only a drunk," heavy-shoulders said. "Kick his ass outa here."

The lanky tough took several steps, grabbed Ki by the arm and shoved him along as Ki protested, "Lemme 'lone! Hey, stoppit!" He pulled away, and suddenly the lanky thief coughed, coughed again and went to his knees.

The other tough turned. "Whassa matter?" He took a step, astonished as his partner fell on his face.

Ki said, "Hey!"

The big man looked up, and a *shuriken* tore out his throat. He fired his pistol into the sky as he fell backward to sprawl in the dirt.

It was all over in seconds.

Terrance O'Toole had been hit in the side by a bullet, but Patrick was untouched. He knelt by his brother. "We got to get him to a doc—"

Terrance coughed dramatically and said, "Put me in the goddamn carriage, Pat."

Ki ripped the injured man's shirt and wrapped it around his body. "Hold that in place. We'll lift you up. Which one's your rig?"

70

"I'll get it," Patrick said. He paused. "We owe you something, friend. Those two woulda killed us."

"My friends and I," Ki said, "we owe Kelton something." He retrieved his throwing star, wiping it on the clothes of the fallen man. When Patrick brought the rig around, Ki helped lift Terrance in.

Ki had made two fast friends. ·

Chapter 10

Two hours later, Ki easily eluded the watchers and slipped in through a window of the Bancroft mansion. Everyone was in bed, but when he woke Jessica to report, the others got up as well. They gathered in the small sitting room around a midnight snack as Ki related what had happened at the Gold Dust Saloon gambling room.

"The O'Toole brothers!" Melissa said. "They belong to a huge family. There must be dozens of them! Kelton has made a terrible enemy!"

Worthy grinned. "And Ki's made some great friends."

Jessica said, "I would like very much to have a look at Kelton's gambling rooms."

"I'll take you," Worthy said at once.

Melissa said, "Why walk into the lion's den?"

"Something might turn up." Jessica smiled, her green eyes twinkling in the lamplight. "And the more you can learn about your enemy, the better prepared you are."

Melissa looked puzzled. "But won't he learn about you, too?"

"Not the right things," Jessie said.

Ki changed the subject. "What about Carlos? Have either of you heard from him?" He looked from Worthy to Melissa.

"No," Melissa answered. "But Garfield is going to the old market again tomorrow. He should learn something."

"Have the police been back here?" Ki asked.

Melissa shook her head. "No, but they're still watching the house day and night."

Ki said, "This is a big house. Can't you make a secret nook here somewhere so Carlos can stay among friends? He'd be a lot safer here than outside where the police might accidentally find him."

Jessica agreed. "He wouldn't have to stay in the hiding place all the time. Only when the police search. It would make Juanita feel better, too."

"And me, too," Melissa said. "I'll talk to Garfield about it in the morning. If anyone should know of a hiding place in this house, Garfield would." She sighed deeply. "I think you're taking too much of a chance to go to Kelton's gambling hall, Jessie. He's a ruthless man."

"We'll watch ourselves," Jessica said. She smiled at Ki. "We've seen his kind before."

Jessica wore a strapless gold lamé gown that was so tight fitting, it hugged her every curve all the way to her knees, then flared out to the floor. Her matching shoulder-length gloves drew the eye to her voluptuous breasts accentuated by the tautness of the material. Worthy said it quite took his breath away, and he was sure no one would be able to gamble while she was in the room.

Jessie was delighted, seeing herself in the full-length mirror. So seldom did she get the opportunity to dress in feminine finery! Most days she wore shirt and jeans, just as the men did. To be able to drape a floor-length sable stole over her shoulder felt simply heavenly. And the look on Worthy's face made it all worthwhile.

When Garfield saw her, his eyes bugged and he opened and shut his mouth like a fish before he could find the words and get them out: "Miss J-Jessica, M-master Worthy . . . t-the carriage is o-outside."

Worthy laughed, and Jessica took his arm.

Melissa primped Jessie's hair and fluffed the stole, watching appreciatively as her friend and her brother descended the front steps as if royalty. "Have a wonderful time, you beautiful people," she called after them. "But be careful!" she couldn't help but add.

Ki rode up on a gray horse just as they climbed into the carriage, and he stayed behind them all the way to the saloon. No one keeping an eye on Worthy even noticed Ki; all eyes that were not on Worthy were on Jessica's splendor. Ki watched the couple get down from their vehicle in front of the Gold Dust Saloon, then he tied the gray to the hitchrack in front while a lad took the carriage around to the alley lot.

At the head of the stairs, Ki saw Jessie and Worthy enter the private gambling rooms, where he could not follow. He wandered into the public rooms and kept an eye on the door. He had promised Jessica's father to look after her, and even with Worthy there, he was on guard.

Jessica's entrance turned all heads.

Without appearing to, she saw the women's eyes narrow at the sight of her and the men's grow wide. It grew almost silent in the room, except for the whir of the roulette wheel, the shuffling of cards, and the soft hum of the overhead fans. In a moment, every man in the house was smiling. No one gave Worthy a second glance.

Slowly Jessie made her way across the room, with her arm linked in Worthy's and her sable stole dragging behind her on the plush oriental rug. A woman nearby took in a deep, audible breath; a tuxedo-clad man on the other side of the room cleared his throat emphatically. People made way for her at the roulette table, and she sat, with Worthy at her back.

The croupier, generally blasé, having seen everything, fumbled with his stick, almost forgetting to make his calls. Then he firmed his lips and shook off her impelling image. "Ladies and gentlemen, put your bets down, please."

Jessie made a few bets and broke even, then got up as the men around the table sighed. Worthy picked up the chips, and they moved on. She played a round of Twenty-One and won as the dealer dropped the cards he was shuffling, spilling them all over the floor and creating a misdeal.

Then Josiah Kelton appeared.

One of the waiters had told him a fabulous lady was in the

gaming room, and he hurried to see her. Perhaps she was one of the actresses from some traveling theatre group.

She was the most ravishing creature he had ever seen! And he was sure he had seen them all! And a stranger to him! Certainly she was no actress; she wore no unnecessary makeup, no jewels. Pure blinding natural beauty, with a glow from within. And those huge eyes, too. But she was with Worthy Bancroft! Was she a relative come to town? Or was she visiting royalty?

Worthy introduced them, and Kelton bowed, as if he really were a gentleman, and kissed her gloved hand. He had never done that before in his life. But somehow he felt compelled. Her name was Jessica Starbuck. Where had he heard that name before?

"Your presence graces my poor house," Kelton said, almost simpering.

"You're very kind, sir," Jessie said sweetly, breathily.

"Are you staying long in our city?"

"That depends," she said provocatively, giving him her best smile and leaning toward him slightly.

His cheeks flushed, and he blinked self-consciously. Then Kelton snapped his fingers at a waiter. "Bring champagne."

The man scurried, hearing his employer's urgency. He was back in a moment with a silver tray and three filled glasses.

Kelton handed them around, raising his in a toast. "To the most beautiful lady San Francisco has ever seen!"

Jessica laughed demurely as Kelton and Worthy sipped the bubbly.

Worthy glanced around the room. Kelton had not looked at him once. Nor had anyone else, he was sure. On the far side of the room, near the faro tables, he spotted Carlotta Reardon, Kelton's mistress. Her face was a mask of hatred! If looks could kill, both Jessica and Kelton would be lying dead on the floor.

As he watched Carlotta, she gathered up her skirts and strode briskly to the door and through it.

Kelton exchanged a few more words with Jessie, then bowed himself away as if taking his leave of royalty.

Jessica looked after him, smiling. Then she turned to Worthy. "He's an oily one, isn't he?"

"Worse than that," Worthy said. "He's a rattlesnake. How long do we have to stay here? Have you seen everything you want?"

"Well, it is smoky in here, isn't it?" Half the men were puffing away on large cigars, and the ceiling fans did not move the air adequately.

"Are you sure you've seen everything you wanted to see? You don't have to leave just on my account."

"I know." She nodded. "Yes, I'm ready to go."

"Then I'll have the carriage brought around."

Kelton went straight from the gaming room to his office. He found Carlotta there waiting for him. She was furious. "Who was that person!?"

"What person?"

She screamed, "You know damn well what person! I saw you kiss her hand! You've never done that to me in your life! You—you—"

He laughed at her. "You're not a lady. I took you outa the orphanage and kept you from having to go to work at Madam Nelsen's. Or have you forgotten?"

She turned pale and swung her fist at him. He easily evaded it and slapped her so hard she fell back against the wall and slid to the floor, sobbing.

He kicked her feet. "Damn it, get up! Get outa here! I got work to do."

She screamed at him again and fought him as he tried to lift her. He yanked her to her feet and shoved her through the open door, slamming it behind her. He swore violently.

Then he sent for Grady.

When the hulking man appeared, Kelton sat him down. "Worthy Bancroft is in the gaming room with a woman."

Grady grinned evilly. "I heard about her, boss. Ever'body's talkin' about her."

"Well, it's Worthy I want. What about a rifle shot when they're in their carriage?"

"No guarantee it won't hit her."

Kelton frowned, rubbing his jaw. If a shot killed her, it would be big news, a gorgeous woman like that! And it might even get back to him. Was it common knowledge yet that he and the Bancrofts were on the outs? There had been rumors, he knew. If it did get back to him, could he cover it up sufficiently to keep from hanging?

Grady said, "What you want me t'do, boss?"

Kelton walked away from him. "I'm thinking!" *It might not be such a good idea to kill Worthy when he's leaving here. The newspapers might just make a connection. And there are still a few honest policemen. . . .*

He turned back to Grady and shook his head. "Let Worthy go. This time. Forget it." He waved the man out.

Melissa took great pains in planning for her party. She sent out invitations to all the celebrities in The City. Starbuck was a well-known and respected name even as far west as San Francisco, so having Jessica Starbuck as her guest of honor was quite a coup. If she and Jessie put their heads together, they could possibly kill two birds with one stone.

Jessie said, "Invite all the people who knew your father back in the old days, when he was a prospector. Is that at all possible?"

"I don't know. We can try." Melissa went about making up a list. "I'm inviting the Comstock 'Silver Kings' and their wives. Father was one of them, you know. Also the Big Four railroad families—the Stanfords, the Hopkins, the Huntingtons, and Crockers. And, of course, everyone else who's anyone in The City."

"An impressive list. Will they all come?"

"If they're in town, I'm sure they will. There would be no reason for them not to attend. Our families have been friends for years. Let's see, we'll have a reception first. I want them all to meet you."

Jessica beamed. "Then I can dress up again!"

"Yes, in your very best."

Jessie laughed. "I'll wear my diamonds! I haven't had this much fun in a long time!"

•　•　•

The formal reception was planned for five o'clock in the afternoon. Carriages began arriving just after five. Garfield had hired half a dozen sturdy lads to handle the horses and rigs. The distinguished guests, all formally attired, came up the walk and were greeted at the door by Garfield, who announced each guest dramatically.

In the reception line just inside the large foyer stood Melissa, Worthy, and Jessie. Melissa and Worthy received their guests warmly, welcomed them, and then proudly introduced each to Jessie.

A long bar had been set up and a group of musicians were playing softly behind a figured screen.

"His Honor, Mayor Cloyd Kimball and Mrs. Kimball," droned Garfield in his best British accent.

Mayor Kimball and his wife, Anita, approached Melissa with broad smiles. The mayor pressed her hand. "Melissa, how lovely you look. How is your dear mother?"

"She is much better, thank you. She improves each day, but she will always be confined to her bed. She's sleeping now."

"Please give her our regards."

"I will. Thank you, Cloyd, Anita." Turning to her brother, she said, "You remember my brother, Worthy?"

Worthy extended his hand to Mrs. Kimball, kissing her hand elegantly. Then he shook the mayor's hand firmly. "Good to see you again, Mayor, Mrs. Kimball. I would like to present Miss Jessica Starbuck, our houseguest from Texas. Jessica, Mayor and Mrs. Kimball."

Jessie smiled sweetly and made eye contact with both of them. "Indeed a pleasure to meet you."

Neither Leland Stanford nor Collis Huntington was able to attend; both sent their sincere regrets. Stanford, he wrote in a long note, was engrossed in a photographic experiment with a man named Muybridge. Huntington had a previous business engagement in Kansas City. . . .

Charles Crocker arrived with his wife and Mrs. Hopkins, the widow of the late Mark Hopkins. Mrs. Hopkins was well-jeweled. Crocker sported a large bushy goatee and was accompanied by a tiny bird-like wife who appeared more than a little nervous when introduced to Jessie.

Crocker's eyes seemed rather hard, Jessie thought as he bowed over her hand.

"Charmed, Miss Starbuck."

Did Mrs. Crocker take offense to his lingering just a little too long over her hand? Or was the woman just high-strung?

After all the guests had arrived, Garfield and the other help passed among them with champagne. So many people clustered around Jessie were totally uninterested in Garfield's wine that he finally gave up trying to provide them with special service and concentrated on the other guests.

"I haven't seen you in San Francisco before, Miss Starbuck, uh, may I call you Jessica?"

"Are you staying long?"

"May I show you the sights of our fair city?"

Melissa finally rescued her friend. "I'm so glad you're here, Mrs. Hopkins. Your husband knew my father well back in the old days, didn't he?"

"He knew him then, yes, Melissa, but not well, I'm afraid. He, uh, only came into frequent contact much later in life, after they both built on the Hill."

Melissa turned to Crocker. "You knew Father as a prospector, didn't you, Mr. Crocker?"

Crocker tugged at his goatee and shook his head solemnly. "You should ask Fred Madison that. I believe W.R. and Fred worked the same part of the territory, if I'm not completely mistaken. Right, Freddie?"

Madison agreed. A short, dumpy man with large hands, he nodded quickly and beamed at Jessica, barely acknowledging Melissa. Eager to please, his eyes flitted as he spoke. "Why, yes. We worked the same area, W.R. and I did. But not the same claims, of course. I do believe he had partners."

"Partners?" Melissa asked, leaning closer to him. "Would you happen to remember their names, Mr. Madison?" Both she and Jessica held their breath.

Madison frowned and shook his head. "It's been a very long time, you know." He obviously wanted desperately to please the gorgeous guest of honor, but his memory failed him. He cleared his throat and looked down at his feet.

Another man, Jim Fair, spoke up, his gaze rarely leaving Jessica. "I remember W.R. in Virginia City, and I agree with Freddie, here. W.R. most certainly had partners. But so did we all. It was nothing all that unusual; there was too much work as a rule for one man alone."

Melissa asked hopefully, "Do any of you gentlemen know a man with a limp?"

Hopkins smiled. "My dear young lady, since the war a great many men limp or have only one leg. I dare say, what a curious question."

Melissa sighed. "Yes, I suppose it is."

Jessica looked from one man to another, batting her long lashes.

Garfield came to the doorway. "Dinner is served!"

Worthy could not keep his eyes off Jessica. His pulse raced at the sight of her. Not only was she beautiful, but she had a delightful sense of humor and displayed marvelous poise. Far from being intimidated by such famous people as the mayor, the chief of police, millionaires and tycoons, she wrapped them all around her little finger. Indeed, she had even won over the wives, a difficult task at best, considering their initial reaction to her extreme beauty.

He wondered if she had been dealing with such eminent people all her life; it appeared so from her comfortable demeanor. He must question Missy more closely about this later.

He had already found her to be a crack shot and brave as a lioness; she could think faster on her feet than anyone he knew. And she was the most sensual woman he had ever seen. He ached with passion. The memory of her burned deep within him, which was annoying in the midst of this party.

He wrenched his mind from her for a few seconds, reminding himself that this evening was planned strictly to gain information about W.R.'s killer. He shook himself and slipped upstairs to look in on his mother. She was sleeping peacefully.

At dinner, Jessica was seated between Chief Granville and Mayor Kimball. Across the table from her was Conrad Hutchinson, who stared at her with calf eyes and ignored the

80

young women on either side of him. Conrad, "Connie" Jessica had called him, much to his delight, was the son of a Bancroft family friend, Councilman Bert Hutchinson. Bert was at the far end of the table, opposite him was his wife, Agatha.

Worthy, seated at the head of the table, found himself annoyed at Conrad's stare; but Jessie, who must have been aware of the young man's gaze, paid the obviously smitten fellow no attention whatsoever. Instead, she hung on her dinner partners' every word. Worthy knew she had the power to make people feel as if they were the most clever conversationalists in the world and their thoughts riveting.

But once in a while she glanced over at Worthy, her smile broadening and her eyes twinkling.

For Worthy, the dinner dragged on and on. He engaged in desultory conversation with his two table companions, hearing half what each said, nodding now and then, wishing he could be alone with Jessie. What would he say to her? Would he have to speak at all? They could take up where they left off the other night. His loins began to burn, and he changed his train of thought and listened for a minute to Mrs. Kimball's recipe for Irish whiskey fruitcake.

Lucinda Barker, daughter of the *San Francisco Bulletin's* owner and publisher and one of Melissa's debutante friends, paid rapt attention to Mrs. Kimball's list of ingredients, forgetting for the moment that she had set her cap for Worthy and was doing her best to entice The City's most eligible bachelor. Worthy leaned back and let his two dinner companions chat cozily.

The party finally came to an end, and guests began to shrug into cloaks and furs and send servants for carriages. Jessica's circle of admirers slowly diminished, Conrad Hutchinson being the very last and most reluctant. But he too finally kissed her hand and tottered off into the night.

Jessica smiled her last smile and, with a long sigh, headed for the small sitting room. "I haven't had an evening like that in years," she said to Melissa.

"Neither have we. I only wish Daddy could have been here. He would have—"

Jessie interrupted, "I was surprised that no one really knew him well as a prospector."

Worthy joined them. "Well, as they all said, it was a long time ago. And you can't get away from it; memories do have a way of fading, given enough time."

Melissa said, "I wish Daddy had kept a journal or some sort of a diary."

"Maybe he didn't want us to know how hard a life it was for him," Worthy said.

"He was terribly closemouthed." Melissa sighed, then smiled at Jessica. "You were simply magnificent! You must have received a hundred invitations tonight."

Jessie laughed modestly. "I can't remember any of them. But now, if no one objects, I think I'll go up to bed. It's been quite a day."

"A very good idea," Worthy said, rising. "I intend to do the very same thing." His crooked smile spoke his true intentions for him.

"Before you go up, there is one last thing I must tell you," Melissa said. "Garfield and I put our heads together, and we've decided on a place where Carlos can hide if the police search the house again. There's room in the pantry behind the big cracker barrel, a room Daddy made for drying meats. From the kitchen, the entrance cannot be detected. You have to know it's there in order to spot it," she said proudly.

"Excellent!" Jessie said.

Worthy applauded. "Brava, Missy!"

Melissa continued, "Garfield will meet Carlos tomorrow at the old market, and he can sneak in here tomorrow night."

Jessie nodded. "Good, but I suggest Ki show him how to avoid the watchers. He's done it several times and can protect Carlos should there be any trouble."

Melissa grinned. "Good idea. Now let's all go to bed, shall we?"

Chapter 11

Ki slipped into the Bancroft mansion at midnight and went directly to Jessica's room. She was awake, unable to sleep, and slid out of bed at once. While he waited at the door, she dressed in black jeans and shirt and pulled a dark cap down over her blonde curls.

Ki was determined to investigate Josiah Kelton's offices at the saloon. He had brought two horses for them, knowing they would never be able to get horses from the Bancroft stable without alerting the police. Ki led the way, out the window, along a hedgerow, over a fence, and along a drainage ditch, avoiding the bored guards who were talking, smoking, and making their positions easily known.

Ki and Jessie rode down the hill and went straight to Kelton's saloon. The place was still open, and the gambling rooms were occupied; but the offices were dark.

They tied their horses a short distance away and walked to the rear of the building. It was easy to climb, Ki said. If they had to, they would break a pane of glass to get in.

But that was not necessary. Ki climbed up first and found that several of the upper-story windows had been left unlocked. Ki pushed a window up and slid over the sill, reaching out to give Jessie a hand.

It was dark inside the room. Jessica found a kerosene lamp; the chimney was still warm. Ki pulled the drapes across the windows, and she struck a match, lighting the wick. They were in an office, but not Kelton's.

"It's the next one," Ki said. He led the way, holding the lamp ahead of him to light the way. Kelton's office door was locked, but Ki had brought along a small steel pry bar. He inserted it into the crack of the door by the lock and pulled. The door frame gave way, and they stepped inside.

Jessica pulled the drapes over the two windows, and they brought the lamp in, setting it on Kelton's desk. The office safe was locked and too formidable for them. Ki went through several cabinets while Jessie searched the desk.

"Nothing here," Ki said in disgust. "The man keeps no records."

Jessie held up a slip of paper. "Here's something, a note about Chicago."

Ki looked at it. "Someone is supposed to meet someone else in Chicago."

"Is that the date Worthy stopped over there?"

Ki smiled. "I think you've hit it. *J.D. meet the 4:50 westbound.* Who's J.D.?"

"One of the men Worthy fought with on the train, I would imagine."

Ki nodded. He put the paper in his pocket and went back to the cabinets. In a few minutes he shook his head. "There's nothing here to connect Kelton to W.R. in any way. If they had dealings, Kelton kept the proof in his head or wrote it down and put it in the safe."

Jessie stared at the squat, black safe. It was far too heavy for them to lift. She was just about to say something when Ki grabbed her wrist.

"Shhh!" he whispered, turning down the lamp.

Jessica froze as heavy booted footsteps clomped down the hall, approaching the office. She was just about to blow out the lamp when the footsteps receded down the stairs.

Ki smiled. "Close call."

Jessie sighed. "Well, I guess we're through here, anyway."

"Yes. Blow out the lamp." He went to the windows.

Opening a window, Ki climbed down first and jumped to

the ground. Jessie slid over the sill and was halfway down the side of the building when someone shouted.

In the next second, a bullet spanged off the wood siding just above her head.

Dressed all in black, she was hard to see, and that fact saved her. She scrambled down and fell into Ki's waiting arms as more bullets ripped into the building and several men shouted for Dave and Hank to hurry up!

Jessie gritted her teeth as she ran, following Ki to the horses. They had undoubtedly run into a roving patrol that guarded the buildings.

The shouts behind them stopped for a minute or two, then came again. Someone was giving orders.

Jessie and Ki reached their horses, and in another moment were galloping down the main street away from the saloon. Rifle shots followed them, but none even came close.

After a few minutes, they reined in and Ki said, "They didn't recognize us. It was too dark."

"Maybe Kelton keeps his important records at home. Where does he live?"

"Melissa will know."

"I'll ask her in the morning."

Melissa received a note by messenger; it was from Bert Hutchinson, asking her to lunch. She replied that she would be delighted.

He came by for her in a black and red carriage, and they rode to the financial district to Tadich's Grill for seafood. Being a councilman, Hutchinson was well known and received the best table in the house.

When they were seated, he said, "I've been extremely worried, Melissa . . . about you and Worthy."

"Why?"

"Well, I was talking to W.R. shortly before the accident and I believe, thinking back, that there was something very wrong. W.R. kept asking me about wills."

"Wills? I thought Father had drawn up his will years ago."

"He wanted to know what was legal and what wasn't. He

wanted to be sure the will for his family would supersede any other document."

Melissa was quite surprised. "What other document?"

"That's just it. I don't know. I'm afraid your father was very secretive about his personal affairs. I was unable to draw out the reasons behind his questions. Now I wish I had pressed him harder. Hindsight, you know."

She nodded. "Yes. And it's true that Father did keep things to himself."

"I got the impression there was a document or two somewhere that worried him. What do you know of his early life in the mines?"

"Unfortunately, very little."

Hutchinson nodded. "I do know that he was in Washoe for a while before striking it rich near Virginia City. That's about all any of us knows. I don't suppose your mother might—"

She shook her head solemnly.

"I suppose there might be someone still living there who could remember," he said.

Melissa said, "That sounds like a very long chance."

"Of course, but I remember a long time ago. When W.R. and I used to get together now and then for a few drinks and some idle chatter, he would reminisce about some man he called Archie." He leaned closer. "Does that name mean anything to you, Missy?"

"Archie? I . . . I don't think so."

"Apparently, they were close."

Melissa thought about the mystery man. "Did this Archie have a limp. Did Father ever mention a limp?"

"Not that I remember."

Garfield went to the old market with his shopping bags as had been planned. He bought spices and bargained with the peddlers. Near the end of the day, Carlos Ortega pulled him by the elbow into the shadows of a stall.

"Miss Melissa wants you to come home," Garfield told him. "We have a secure hiding place in the house for you. I can assure you, you will be much better off and safer there."

Carlos nodded. "Si, I will come."

"Do you know who Ki is?"

"Si, he followed you last time and introduced himself. Then he hurried away, afraid his being a stranger would attract attention."

"He will meet you tonight by the old lighthouse and will guide you into the house. The police will never suspect. He slips in and out at will."

Carlos nodded vigorously. He would soon see his Juanita. "I will be there. *Gracias, amigo.*"

Carlos met Ki long after dark at the lighthouse. Ki had two horses, and they rode to a grove of trees near the mansion, where they got down.

Ki said quietly, "We will leave the horses here."

Ki led the way along a drainage ditch, over a fence, and along a hedgerow, avoiding the guards. He opened a basement window, and they slid inside. Melissa and Juanita met them when they went upstairs.

"Carlos!" Juanita flew into her husband's arms.

Jessica appeared, and joined Ki and Melissa for coffee in the sitting room while Carlos and his wife embraced and talked in the hallway. Carlos looked very well for a hunted man, they agreed.

When Carlos and Juanita finally came into the sitting room, he explained that at first he had stayed with a distant cousin, and then moved from one place to another frequently. He had had no trouble at all from the police. He thanked Melissa for the money, saying it had saved his life. He had been able to buy clothes and food and pay for his secret lodgings. He smiled. Even his cousin was more inclined to help when there was money to be had.

They sat him down, as Juanita excused herself to prepare for bed, and asked him about the accident. "Tell us what you can remember," said Ki.

Carlos frowned, thinking back. He had listened to W.R. and Señora Bancroft arguing in the back of the carriage on the way to and from the party.

"What was the argument about?"

"Señora Bancroft did not want to go to the Señor Kelton's dinner. She wanted to know what business her husband could have with such a man. She wanted Señor Bancroft to share his troubles with her."

"And then what?"

"There was much fog, more than usual, I think. I hear voices, but I do not see anyone."

"Children's voices?" Melissa asked.

Carlos shrugged. "How could they be children? But small men, maybe."

"What about the giggles?"

"Si, I hear the giggles. I remember them later. Someone scare the horses. They bolt and run at the barrier." Carlos shook his dark head. "I cannot understand how they break through it."

Melissa said to Ki and Jessie, "The police told us the barrier had not been sawed. But it must have been."

Carlos nodded.

Jessie said, "Then the police lied, or someone took away the sawed ends."

Worthy agreed. "It would have been easy enough to do."

Melissa asked Carlos, "Have you ever seen a man around here with a limp?"

"Si, Señorita."

"Where?"

"This man come here to the house. He is old, with a cloak so I could not see his face. Your father let him in through the back door."

"Did they know you saw them?"

Carlos shook his head.

"Then you do not know who he is?"

"No. I am sorry."

Melissa went with Carlos then, to show him the hiding place she and Garfield had devised. He must get into it at once if the police appear. In fact, he must never stray too far from it, so he would be able to get into it in time. She suggested that Juanita could stay in the house, in one of the cook's rooms in the servants' quarters rather than over the stable. He rushed off to be with his wife.

When Melissa returned to the sitting room, the four discussed what Carlos had told them. Someone had most certainly spooked the horses deliberately, and cut the barrier so it would give way.

Jessica said, "Who else knew the Bancrofts would be coming that particular night, but Kelton?"

"No one," Worthy agreed. "But can we prove it?"

Jessica sighed deeply. "Possibly not."

Ki took his leave of the others, returned to the two picketed horses, and rode back to the Nugget Hotel.

Jessica went to bed thinking about Carlotta, Kelton's mistress. *She might have some damaging information in her digs.* It was worth a try.

Since neither Melissa nor Worthy knew where Kelton lived, and it was too difficult for Carlos to put into English the directions, Ki found it necessary to follow Kelton home, not an impossible task. Josiah Kelton lived on a hill in a house designed for security. It had only a nominal fence around it, but there were no plants or trees or shrubs anywhere around the house, which was in the center of an expanse of lawn. There was no cover at all for an approaching man. At night, there were lanterns around the house to light the grounds, and men patrolled constantly.

Ki shook his head at it. Kelton apparently had something to hide. And he had made sure that no one would get into that house without an invitation.

It took Ki another day to follow Carlotta Reardon to her home. She lived in an older house in a central part of The City, but she was seldom home. However, she had a housekeeper, a maid, and a stableboy.

Ki entered the house at midnight and spent many minutes learning the layout. The housekeeper, he discovered, was the only servant who stayed there all night. She slept in a downstairs room near the kitchen. He listened at her door, then went upstairs quickly and lighted a lantern in Carlotta's bedchamber. It held a four poster, a large chest of drawers, and a long table with mirrors. Beside the bed was a locked chest, which took all of five minutes to open with his knife.

Inside were papers and a diary. The papers were apparently of little interest. He put the diary in his pocket.

Chapter 12

Worthy was extremely annoyed with Melissa when he discovered she had gone to lunch with Bert Hutchinson. "You must not leave this house! Is that clear! It is far too dangerous! Jessie and Ki told you that. Why wouldn't you listen?"

"But nothing happened."

"It is foolish to argue. You must not leave this house under any circumstances, Missy, unless you're accompanied by either Jessie or Ki. Do you understand? Of course, I thought you understood before, when they first warned you."

Melissa knew her brother was right, but nothing had happened since those attempts on Worthy, first in Chicago, then on the train, and then at the lighthouse. And no one could say for certain that they had not simply been robbers after his money.

The household had settled down a bit. Carlos was home again, though he dared not show his face outside. Juanita, using the excuse that she was lonely and frightened living over the stable with Carlos gone, had moved into the main house. Now, with Carlos hiding behind the kitchen, she was able to be with him all the time.

Dr. Witherspoon came to the house twice a week to look in on Penelope. She was able to sit up, after a fashion, and her mind had cleared a good bit. Enough so that she demanded from time to time to speak with W.R. But Worthy had told her that W.R. was in the East on business, and she fretted.

"When is he coming back?"

"Whenever his business allows him."

"But it's been too long already. . . ."

"Mother, it just seems a long time because you miss him, that's all," Worthy lied.

Dr. Witherspoon was afraid that a severe shock, such as her finding out that W.R. was dead, might upset her far too much, might even push her sanity over the brink. He insisted that it would be much better to keep the information from her, at least for the time being. Of course, one day she would have to know. One day when she was physically and emotionally stronger and could accept such knowledge.

Jessica remained in the house, too, and Ki came in by way of his secret paths to confer with the others. He had been keeping a watch on Kelton, but had learned very little. It was one thing to watch someone's movements and quite another to listen to his conversations. That, of course, was impossible.

The most interesting topic of discussion with Jessica, Ki, Worthy, and Melissa was the diary Ki had stolen from Carlotta Reardon's home. Beside the usual personal entries, it was also filled with names and figures. But these pages were in a code that they had not yet deciphered. While Ki was out on surveillance, Worthy, Jessica, and Melissa spent hours poring over the diary, filling sheets of paper with endless possibilities.

Jessica had been considering something else quite seriously, and when Ki appeared late that night, she talked it over with him. "I think we should go to Virginia City."

Ki nodded. "And ask about W.R.'s early life and his mining partners."

"Exactly. All his enemies later in life were merely of a political nature, none of them murderous. It was something from his wild days as a prospector that came back to haunt him, I would suspect."

Ki nodded again in agreement. "When do you want to go dredge up W.R.'s past?"

"Why not tomorrow?"

"Good!"

* * *

Jessica and Ki sneaked out early the following morning after letting Worthy and Melissa know where they intended to go. They slipped past the watchers just before dawn and were on their way. They went first to Sacramento, a good two days' ride from San Francisco, and spent a couple of days there asking questions. The few old-timers they could locate who were still around Sutter's Mill and the gold area were of almost no help, and they learned very little from them. A few remembered W.R., but too much time had passed. In those days, W.R. had been only one among tens of thousands toiling in the gold fields. There had not been that much to set W.R. apart from all the others.

Ki and Jessica continued on into the foothills of the Sierra Nevadas, winding their way up toward the infamous Donner Pass. They made slow progress once they passed the tree line, and the horses labored up the mountainside. Their one big consolation was that they had nothing to fear from Indians in California or Nevada. All known tribes were friendly.

They marveled at the beauty of Tahoe, a lake created by melting Sierra snows, and headed for the deserts beyond. They continued on the trail to Virginia City and arrived in the middle of the day. They put up at the Silverado Hotel, and Jessica looked forward to a nice hot tub to cleanse off the road dust.

The hotel desk clerk was an older man with steelrimmed glasses and white hair. "Howdy. You two been riding a piece, ain't ya?"

"Yes," Jessie said, stomping the dust off her boots.

As they registered, Ki asked, "Were you here during the Rush?"

The old man smiled broadly. "I come here in late '49, and I'm still here."

"But you didn't strike it rich?"

"Damn few did, I'll tell you. But I made some good finds. 'Course in them days, the money went out fast, too. We were young, and it was gonna last forever."

Ki said, "Did you ever know a man named Worthington Bancroft, some called him W.R.?"

He rolled the full name over his tongue. "Worthington

93

Bancroft, that's a pretty hefty handle." Then he shook his head. "Nope, I'd have remembered someone with a name like that. But you might ask old Matt Clayton. He kept track of things better'n most."

"Where would I find him?"

"You might try the Brass Ring. If he's not there, try all the saloons in town. Ever'body knows 'im." He handed them their room keys.

"Thanks."

Josiah Kelton received a wire from Virginia City. Dalton Fisher, one of Kelton's freighting managers, wired that two people—a knockout blonde cowgirl and a big Chinaman— were asking pertinent questions about W.R. Bancroft's early mining days. Did this mean anything to Kelton?

Kelton wired back immediately that it most certainly did. The two were big trouble and must be stopped. He suggested —in code—that someone take care of the matter at once and permanently.

Kelton was more short-tempered than anyone in his employ had ever seen him, and he had never been known for gentleness. He shouted that he was surrounded by idiots and fools. Someone had ransacked his office, and someone had searched Carlotta's home. Carlotta reported to him that nothing had been taken from her place, but the very fact that there had been break-ins was quite distressing, and a little unnerving.

He had no idea who the dirty culprit might be, but it was curious that he'd had no such problems before Worthy Bancroft returned home from back East. Was Worthy capable of such second-story work? Grady had reported what a good shot he was; but Grady and Zack had also reported that no one had gone in or come out of the Bancroft house without their knowledge. If it wasn't Worthy, then who the hell was it?

Kelton brooded about that. How could Grady and Zack be so positive that no one could get past their surveillance?

Carlos Ortega had also evaded his clutches. Search as they might, Kelton's men had been completely unable to turn up the man. No one had seen him or heard a word about him since he ran from the police at the cemetery. The man had disappeared into thin air. How could that be? It was more than just a little frustrating. Kelton fumed.

Bart and Clint, the two bartenders at the Brass Ring Saloon knew old Matt Clayton well, they said. But neither of them had seen him for a day or two.

"He isn't in town all the time, miss," Clint said to Jessie. "He just comes in to visit and wet his whistle."

"Of course, sometimes he nearly drowns in it," added Bart with a straight face.

"Why don't you ride by his shack? It's only a few miles out of town," said Clint, ignoring Bart.

"Which way?"

Clint said, "Take the road north till you come to the old adobe on the left. It's the only house you'll see."

Bart said, "There's a trail that leads left to the creek. Old Matt's place is right there by the creek. You can't miss it."

"Thank you."

Letting their own mounts rest from the long ride, Ki and Jessica got horses from the livery stable and followed the bartenders' instructions. The adobe was a falling-down hovel where no one lived. A trail led westward from it, and as they came to the creek, they saw a shack. A burro was munching grass in front; it looked at them without interest and went right on eating. A gray cat sat in the doorway and yawned as they got down and approached.

Ki said loudly, "Anybody home?"

An old man stuck his white-haired head out the door. "Who zat?"

"Friend," Ki said.

The old man looked at Jessie and smiled broadly, a toothless grin. "Well, I done gone to heaven. Look what come t'see old Matt!"

Jessica smiled and held out her hand. "Hello, Mr. Clayton. You are Matt Clayton, aren't you?"

"Yup." Matt took Jessie's outstretched hand in his after first rubbing it clean on his pants. He was a short, bewhiskered man wearing clothes that should have been thrown away

95

ages ago. He looked up at Jessie with little watery eyes. "Land! I ain't seen nobody like you in—hell, in fifty years!"

Ki asked, "Who'd you see fifty years ago to match her?"

Matt looked at him. "M'baby daughter, Zoe." He sighed deeply. "Ain't much of a comparison, hey? What-all you folks doin' way out here? An' how'd you know m'name?"

"We asked in town," Jessie said. "Everybody in Virginia City knows you."

"Guess they does at that. I been here longer'n just about any of 'em." He shook his head. "Nope, longer'n all of 'em put together."

Ki opened the flap of his saddle bags and took out the bottle they'd bought in town for the old man. He handed it over, and Matt's eyes rounded.

"Hellfire! You brought me a present?" He looked at them suspiciously. "What y'all want?"

"Only to ask you a few questions," Jessie said.

"What about?"

"Early times," she said. "Did you know a man named Worthington Bancroft?"

Matt blinked at them in surprise. "W.R.? Hell, yes, I knew 'im. Why? Nobody ever called him by that long handle." Old Matt pointed to boxes on the porch. "Whyn't you sit a spell."

Ki up-ended several boxes, and he and Jessie sat down. Matt sat on a big hunk of log facing them and fished out a corncob pipe. "I ain't even thought about W.R. in a coon's age. How do you come to know of him?"

"He was a schoolmate's father," said Jessie.

"*Was?*" demanded old Matt. "He gone, too?"

Jessie nodded solemnly. "He was killed in a carriage accident. An accident we aren't so sure was an accident."

Old Matt blew out his breath, picked up his cat, and scratched it under the chin. "Damn. One more less," he said to the cat. "Pretty soon none of us'll be here." He sighed again and peered straight into Jessie's eyes. "What you want to know, purty lady?"

"Jessie, and this is my friend, Ki. We'd appreciate anything you can tell us about W.R.'s early days. First of all, did he have partners?"

"Sure he did. We all did, one time or 'nother."

"Do you remember their names?"

Matt squinted, looking toward the creek where white water splashed over rocks, and stroked the cat's back and tail. "Things changed in them days. A man had one partner one day, and another'n the next." He shook his white head. "Nope, I can't put no name to any . . . none of W.R.'s partners, anyway. You gotta remember, they was a thousand men in the silver fields, maybe more. And we was all so busy."

Ki said, "W.R. brought his wife and children out from back East."

"Yup, I heard he did. By then, he'd made hisself a small strike." Matt looked toward the creek again, his eyes moving along it. He pushed the cat off his lap and stood up, shading his eyes.

Ki said, "What is it?"

"Horses. What the hell they doin' over there by the crick?"

Jessie stood. "I don't see anyone."

"Some fellers moseying around." Matt grumbled and sat again to fire up his pipe.

Jessie said, "Mr. Clayton, did you know a man named Josiah Kelton?"

Old Matt threw back his head and laughed loud and long. "Kelton! Hell, yes, what a sonofabitch! Pardon my language, Miss Jessie, but he was a claim-jumper, y'know, and I ain't got no use for the likes o' him!" He stood again, frowning off toward the creek, then ducked inside the shack, reappearing with a rifle in hand.

Ki said, "You know those riders?" He indicated the creek.

Matt shook his head. Raising the rifle, he levered a shell into the chamber and fired a shot into the air.

Almost instantly, five shots came in a burst of rifle fire. Ki flung himself at Jessie and bore her down in the dirt. One shot spanged off the doorway of the shack, splintering the wood at belt height.

Ki rolled and looked toward the creek. He could see two horsemen in the trees at the edge of the stream. One fired three shots as he stared. The shots hit the shack and a pile of wood near it. Then both horsemen turned away and disappeared in the trees.

Ki got up slowly, his eyes on the distant trees.

Jessie gave a little cry and knelt by the old man. She looked up at Ki. "He's dead."

Ki gritted his teeth. "I don't think they were shooting at him."

Jessie stared at him. "Who knows we're here?"

"That wouldn't be hard to find out. But old Matt has lived here for years. They could have shot him any time they wanted if they were after him."

"That's right. So it was us they wanted."

"Kelton has a long arm."

Jessie looked at him. "Kelton."

"Who else?" Ki studied the creek. "Those men were very foolish. They fired from horseback. Maybe they were men someone scrounged up in hopes of doing us harm. They certainly were not professionals."

Jessie shook her head sadly, looking at old Matt Clayton. "They did do us harm. One of us ought to stay here with the body." She walked to her horse and pulled the Winchester from its boot. "I doubt if they'll be back."

"Probably not. I'll ride into town and bring a wagon."

Ki was back with the undertaker's assistant and a buckboard in just a little over two hours. They lifted the body of the old man into the wagon and tied the burro on behind, but no one could find the gray cat.

"He's probably half wild anyhow, and halfway to the next territory by now," the assistant said, urging Jessie and Ki to discontinue their search.

It was a sad procession back into town; they arrived at dusk. A deputy came by and listened to their story, nodding his head. "You didn't get a good look at any of them, did you?"

"Too far away," Ki said. "We had no binoculars. One rode a bay horse, the other a roan. Not much to go on."

The deputy said, "I'll ride out there in the morning, see if old Matt had anything of value in his kick. Too bad . . . too damn bad."

After breakfast the next morning, Jessie and Ki went to the county building and asked about W.R. Bancroft. A clerk found them some yellowing records to search through. Jessie found that a Worthington R. Bancroft had filed a claim with a partner, Archibald Weaver.

"Weaver!" Ki said triumphantly. "That's the first we've heard of a partner."

Jessie said, "What's become of Weaver?"

They sifted through more files of vital statistics and found a notification under *W*: A fire had burned out Archibald Weaver and his entire family. A cabin had burned to the ground. Fire being one of the most common forms of tragedy.

"Go see Wally Beldinger at the newspaper," the county clerk advised. "These records don't tell you much at all, and you might find a story about the item or an obituary at least. Wally is the one to see."

It was excellent advice. The newspaper morgue at the local paper was extensive, presided over by an overweight older woman named Wallis Beldinger, who knew W.R.'s name.

"I've seen a tintype of W.R. Now where was it?" She began to look through cardboard boxes holding copies of early newspapers. It took her well over an hour to locate an item with a photograph of W.R. and another man. The caption read: *Worthy Bancroft and Archie Weaver at Big Nose Creek*.

The news item said that Bancroft and Weaver had sold a claim for an undisclosed amount. Both men were returning to San Francisco with their families to spend the winter in comfort. Each man would be back in the spring to continue mining.

"You know, I seem to remember something about Archie Weaver," said the woman. "No one ever found his assets. There was a mystery surrounding that fire, you know. Let me see if I can find . . ." She went into another box, and then another, until she found what she was looking for. "Yes, here's the story about the tragedy. Archie's wife, Melanie, and child, Charles, died in the fire."

"Wait," said Jessica, "what about Archie?"

The older woman nodded her head, her jowls shaking. "It was never proved that Archie Weaver died in that fire, but he disappeared. So most thought he had perished. A few thought he might have left because of grief and never just come back. Here's a picture of him." Wallis showed them a reproduction from a tintype. Weaver had obviously been an unkempt man, with hair falling over his ears and into his eyes; he wore a large shaggy mustache and had squinty eyes.

On the back of the photo was written his name and the date, and a note that Weaver's left earlobe was missing.

Jessica asked, "Do you remember? Did he limp?"

"Not that I recollect, but if he'd been injured in the fire. . . . For all I know, he's no longer alive," said the woman.

Ki said, "Is there any chance that he would still be alive today, do you think?"

"Well, yes, certainly if he escaped that fire. Of course, he would be in his late seventies now."

Jessie and Ki thanked the woman and went back to the hotel. So Archie Weaver might still be alive. Perhaps he was the mysterious limping man who had been seen around the Bancroft home and who W.R. had let in the house. If so, why? To give him money? They agreed that they just might be jumping to conclusions, but this was their first big lead.

They stopped by and saw the deputy sheriff again late in the afternoon. He had just come back from old Matt Clayton's digs, he said. "But someone was there before me and burned the shack to the ground."

"Damn," said Ki, "and no clues as to who did it?"

The deputy shook his head. There was nothing he had found to go on.

When they were alone, Ki said, "Just because of us. No one bothered that old man till we came along. What could he have that would hurt or threaten anyone?"

Jessica's blonde curls tumbled as she shook her head sadly.

"Someone torched that shack just in case. Old Matt just might have had some old letters."

"I'd like to get my hands on those lousy bushwhackers!"

Jessie smiled. "Well, if they're serious, you might after all. It's a long way back to San Francisco.

Chapter 13

Jessie and Ki went to the livery stable, saddled up their horses, and left early that morning. They agreed that it had been a good idea not to rely on the train or stagecoach. Both could be halted somewhere along the path, and passengers would be trapped inside, easy prey for whoever was gunning for them. On horseback, they could get off the road and make it extremely difficult for anyone to ambush them.

As they were approaching Carson City, traveling south, Ki suggested they stop long enough to check with the U.S. Bureau of Mines. It was just possible that there were existing records of old claims. With any luck...

To their relief, by the time they came within sight of the town, they still had seen no sign of travelers at all. Nevada was a vast and empty land, very sparsely settled, with most settlements and cabins predictably along creeks and near good waterholes.

If someone was waiting for them along the road somewhere, he was still waiting.

The Bureau of Mines offices were in a shabby, green building on a side street. The Bureau obviously had not allotted funds for putting up a front for the public's benefit. The windows had badly scratched gold leaf, and the inside walls showed cracks, doubtless from some forgotten earthquake. There was a musty smell to the place.

When Jessie and Ki made their request to the clerk at the front desk, they were reluctantly given over to a small, bald man with spectacles and a green eyeshade. "How can I help you?" he asked, his gaze lingering on Jessie's blouse while the front clerk kept a wistful eye on the back of her jeans.

Oblivious to the attention being paid her curves, Jessie said, "We're trying to find information on claims held by a Worthington R. Bancroft."

The small man smiled, looking her in the eye. "There can't have been many by that name. Let me see . . ."

He went away, and they heard him humming to himself. After a long while, he was back with a slip of paper and several musty folders.

"Sorry it took so long." He flipped open the top folder. "Bancroft, Worthington Ralston, in all, filed eleven claims." He checked his slip of paper and his finger moved down a form in the second folder. "One claim was his alone. Five were with a partner, one Archibald Weaver, and three with someone listing himself only as H. Kelsey." He turned to the next folder. "Two claims were disputed. No partners are listed on them." He smiled broadly, forcing his eyes to meet Jessie's instead of dipping down to her blouse again.

"The Kelsey claims," said Ki, "were they with Bancroft?"

The clerk looked again, thumbing from one folder to another. Nodding his head, he said, "They were with Bancroft, Weaver, and Kelsey."

They thanked the man and the front clerk and went out into the blinding sunlight and the pine-scented fresh air. They both unconsciously sucked in a deep breath to clear their lungs of the dust and mildew.

"H. Kelsey," Jessie said. "Is that J. Kelton?"

"I wouldn't bet against it."

Jessie and Ki left Carson City early the next morning, before the stores were open, and were far down the trail by midday. They had planned all along to slip on around the southern rim of Lake Tahoe on their way back to San Francisco, just in case their enemies figured they would retrace their route over Donner Pass to the north. The southern route was also not quite as steep and treacherous as the northern trail.

The sun baked down on them, and the scent of pines blended with the spicy fragrance of manzanita bushes. They met several pack trains and individual wagons plodding along. It was a good but rutted road, seeking the easiest path over the mountains to Placerville, once called Hangtown in the wild days. The decent element in the town had risen up and demanded they discard the old name years ago. It was a disgrace, they said.

The very first shot, from the trees, killed Jessie's horse. The animal reared, went to its knees, and rolled over with a bullet between the eyes.

Jessie easily jumped free, grabbed Ki's saddle horn, and hung on as Ki spurred into a ravine and slid off the saddle, pulling his Winchester.

"Persistent," Ki said, flopping on his belly. He pushed the rifle ahead of him and peered in the direction of the ambusher's shot.

Jessie moved to Ki's left a dozen feet and studied the slope across from them closely. There had been three shots in all. Only one had hit the horse. The other two had cracked over her head as she ducked down. Were she and Ki going to have to fight their way back?

Ki whispered, "You hear anything?"

Jessie put her ear to the ground. "Someone's moving away," she said aloud.

"Maybe they decided it was a bad place to get us after all." He stood up. "They missed us with the first shots, and now they're getting out. Probably to ambush us another day."

Jessie asked, "You think it's the same ones who killed old Matt?"

"Probably. Someone has obviously paid them to see that we don't return to San Francisco." He smiled at her. "I wonder who that could be?"

She laughed. "Yes, it is a puzzle, isn't it."

They were forced to leave the saddle. Jessie pulled the blanket-roll off the dead horse and mounted behind Ki as they proceeded more slowly, abandoning the trail and finding their own track through the pines and manzanita.

At nightfall, they had yet to make contact again with the bushwhackers. They found a small, overhanging cliff and made camp under it so that they had only three sides to watch. But no one disturbed them probably, said Ki, because the ambushers could not find them.

As they ate cold meat and drank fresh creek water, they speculated on their enemies. How many were there? When old Matt had been shot, they had seen only two men; but that did not mean there had not been five or ten present. It was unlikely, however, that anyone would pay a large group to eliminate just the two of them. But they were sure they opposed at least two. Two or three, those were comfortable odds.

Before dawn, Jessie and Ki were on the move again.

"If we're lucky," said Ki, "we can get ahead of them and give them the same medicine they gave us."

"Except that they know us and we don't know them."

"That is a small drawback."

Jessie and Ki paralleled the trail, of necessity moving slowly, occasionally returning to the trail to traverse rough areas. They saw no one for several hours. Then the trail dipped down into a wide canyon, and Ki dismounted, motioning for Jessie to join him. He indicated the land ahead of them.

"Perfect for ambush," he said. "We'd make better targets on the horse."

Jessie pulled the Winchester from its boot and levered a shell into the chamber. The sound echoed and bounced across the wide expanse.

"You lead on," she said in a low voice, "and I'll follow at about fifty feet."

Ki nodded and set out through the thick forest, leading the horse. They had gone about a mile when he held up his hand and halted. He came back toward her.

"I saw movement there." He pointed. "I think it was a man on a gray. They were gone in a second."

"Do you think he saw you?"

"I doubt it. They may be waiting for us there," he said, pointing again. "Maybe we can circle them."

"How far away?"

"A quarter of a mile. Too far for them to hear the horse."

Ki went back to his animal and turned toward the left. Jessie followed, and in a few moments they came to a ravine. Ki slid down into it, grinning at her.

The ravine had a sandy bottom; it wound downward, curving and turning back. In a mile or so, it began to widen.

Suddenly Jessie saw Ki run and duck behind a tree bole. There was a shot that chipped bark over Ki's head. She crawled forward, the Winchester ready. More shots followed the first; it seemed as if there were at least three or four men firing at once.

Ki had plopped down and was flat on his stomach, waiting out the storm of lead. Jessie lost sight of him then in the underbrush and moved very slowly toward the shooting. She heard several yells and stood by a large pine, watching. Three men appeared, charging toward Ki.

Jessie raised the rifle and fired off five shots as fast as she could lever. She saw one man knocked sideways, he disappeared in the brush. The other two halted, yelping in surprise. She fired three more times, seeking them out.

Then she ducked down and crawled to her left, closer to Ki. She met him in a moment, and he was grinning broadly.

"They ran like rabbits," he said. "You took them completely by surprise!"

"I think I hit one."

"I know you did."

Jessie and Ki went to look for the unlucky ambusher and found him face down in the weeds. Ki searched the body.

"His name was Pete Haskins. According to these papers, he lived in Virginia City." Ki stood up. "Dressed like a man down on his luck, and he certainly was."

"Someone bought a posse."

"There's only seven dollars in his kick. Shall we keep it?"

Jessica made a face. "We earned it."

Ki smiled. "If we remember, we'll give it to the poor when we get back."

106

They went on cautiously, trailing the departing ambushers. Ki had seen three, he said, counting the unlucky one.

"They'll be very careful from now on."

The tracks were plain on the soft ground; they had tied the horses several hundred yards from the spot where they'd tried to bushwhack Ki, and the tracks showed them galloping away down the valley.

"Brave as lions," Ki said. "I wonder if they were paid first or if they have to bring back our heads."

"If they try to trap us again, it'll mean they have to bring back at least our ears."

Ki nodded. "I think you're right."

It was not the best arrangement, two on a horse, but Jessie and Ki had no choice. The bushwhackers had taken the downed man's horse with them, and they were traveling through a part of the country where there were no settlements, no place to obtain a new mount.

The next ambush came quicker than they had figured. It might have worked, except that Ki's horse whinnied, and instantly Ki was off the animal, pulling Jessie down with him. Shots cracked over their heads, where they had been just seconds before.

The ambushers were behind an outcropping of boulders that had been partially hidden by willows. Jessie had the Winchester, and she crawled toward the right while Ki went left. They might be able to get the bushwhackers in a crossfire.

Thirty feet from the outcropping, Ki paused and tossed stones at the spot where he thought the shooting had come from. The response was immediate and deafening. Wild shots blasted the underbrush, none even coming close.

Jessie rounded the end of the outcropping as Ki continued to toss stones high in the air so they came down rattling among the boulders. She waited, resting the rifle on a rounded granite rock, and in a few moments, two men ran into her line of vision, heading for their horses.

Sighting carefully, she picked off one. He collapsed in a sprawling heap. She kept firing and winged the second man, but he managed to get aboard his horse. However, he had no chance to grab the reins of the second mount. The wounded man was off down the valley toward Nevada with Jessie's shots whizzing about his ears and flicking his shirt.

Ki stood, cheering. "That one'll run all the way back to Virginia City if I'm any judge of character!"

It was a complete victory, and now they had another horse.

Chapter 14

Josiah Kelton scowled at the two Chinese who were pushed into the room by Grady. He pointed to the chairs in front of his desk, and the Asians sat.

Kelton said to Grady, "Have you told them what we want from them?"

"Yeh, boss."

"Did you make positive sure they know?"

"Sure. They know enough lingo."

Kelton regarded the two as he puffed a long cigar. The two were skinny and rather wizened, both wearing loose oriental shirts and pants. They did not impress him.

He leaned over his desk toward them, hands clasped together. "I give you my word. Your wives and children will be sold if you do not do as you are told!"

"We do! We do!" one said quickly, nodding.

Kelton stared at them till they both winced and looked away. Then he motioned to Grady. "Take them out."

Grady herded the two little men into the hall and returned. "When d'you want them to do it, boss?"

"The sooner the better."

"Tonight?"

Kelton shrugged. "Why not?" He frowned at Grady. "I don't want any slip-ups. Those two didn't finish off the Bancroft carriage job."

109

"That was just bad luck, boss. They got the old man, didn't they? They carried away the sawed boards just like you said, didn't they? An' the old lady is paralyzed and almost as good as dead, ain't she? An' Ortega has disappeared. I mean, nobody's seen him since. Maybe he took off for Mexico."

"You're an idiot, Grady. His wife is still there in the Bancroft house."

"Well, maybe they split up."

Kelton waved the man out. "Go see that they do it, and do it right this time."

He sat behind the desk as Grady nodded and shut the door. Why hadn't he heard something from Virginia City? Didn't they know there was a telegraph line? He chewed the cigar. It was a real pain in the ass to have to depend on incompetent underlings all the time.

Well, maybe no news was good news.

Ki and Jessie arrived back in San Francisco early in the evening and split up to go to their respective hotels. She went to the Palace Hotel suite to bathe and change into her feminine attire. Clean, with her hair redone and dressed in a kelly green lace and silk suit, she looked totally different from the jeans-clad rider with the Winchester.

Ki also bathed and changed into a clean shirt and black jeans and vest. By the time he was shaved and ready, Jessie's hack had pulled up to the Nugget Hotel. He hopped on his horse tethered in the alley and followed the hack almost all the way to the Bancroft mansion. He slipped in the basement window while Jessica paid the cabbie.

Melissa and Worthy were surprised and delighted to see them, especially so fresh and clean after such a trip. Once again, they all immediately trooped into the small sitting room to discuss the adventures of the journey. Garfield brought hot chocolate and cookies, then asked if the travelers had eaten.

They admitted they had not, and the old man hurried out to the kitchen to alert the cook.

Jessie said, "First, let us tell you what we learned about your father. He did have partners, two in fact. One was Archibald Weaver, Archie; they were partners for over five

110

years. The other one was a man named H. Kelsey."

"Kelsey!" Worthy exclaimed. "Could that possibly be Kelton?"

"We wondered that, too," Ki said, "but we could find absolutely nothing about him."

"Remember, Bert Hutchinson told me that Father kept reminiscing about someone named Archie!"

"And," Jessie said, "Archie Weaver just may have a limp."

Melissa stared at her. "The man with the limp might be this Archie Weaver? Do you really think it could be? If so, what does he want?"

Jessie shook her head. "We can't be positive that Archie Weaver is even alive. We were told that he and his whole family were burned up in a fire."

"So he's still a mystery man, the man who limps." Melissa sighed deeply. "Will we ever clear this up?"

Worthy smiled at his sister and changed the subject, asking, "Did you have any trouble in Virginia City?"

Ki glanced at Jessie and smiled. "Yes, a bit. Someone who wanted us dead knew we were there. How that happened, we don't know."

"We told no one!" Worthy said quickly.

Melissa shook her head vehemently.

Jessie touched each on the hand. "Of course not."

When the implication of Ki's words sank in, Melissa said, "You mean, you were shot at!?"

"Only a few times," said Ki, suppressing a grin.

The two Chinese coolies employed by Josiah Kelton were taken to the vicinity of the Bancroft mansion. Grady pointed out the house. "There's police guards watching the place, so be very careful." He frowned at them. "Understand?"

They both nodded, and one giggled nervously. They were dressed all in black and had sharp knives in their belts. They had refused the offer of pistols, being unfamiliar with the weapons.

"All right, get on with it," Grady growled. He watched them skuttle away into the darkness. He shook his head. Why Kelton continued to employ those two was a mystery to him.

He thought them quite unreliable. No one could be sure how much they really understood when you talked to them. They constantly nodded their heads as if they knew, but did they? Maybe Kelton felt he could disown them if they got caught.

The two Chinese had come highly recommended to Kelton; their names were Ayako, the older, and Hing. They had been employed by one of their own kind for several years, to keep order among workers. Their swift knives were feared and respected in the vast Chinese community.

But they had never, until Kelton, worked among round eyes, and both Ayako and Hing were wary of them. They thought whites unpredictable, impatient, and prone to unnecessary violence.

Cautiously, they looked over the huge house and expansive grounds, easily determining where the police watchers were; there were four of them. Two were watching the front, and two the back. Ayako led the way past the watchers in the rear of the house and examined the windows of the basement. All were securely locked. He motioned to Hing, who put his padded jacket's elbow through a glass pane. The sound was not as loud as might be expected because he instantly covered the window with his body. Then he picked the glass slivers out, and the two slid inside.

The basement was very dark. They had to feel their way. It took many minutes to cross the room, and they would have lost themselves if they had not had the pale square of the window to keep at their backs.

They found the stairs and crept up silently to the hall door in their cloth shoes. Grady had told them everyone in the house should be asleep at this hour, but they were not. Hing opened the basement door just a crack and listened. He thought he heard voices. Ayako pushed him, and he opened the door wider and stepped out.

There was no lamp in the hallway, but light came from the far end, enough to see by. Ayako pointed, and Hing padded to the end of the hall. He could definitely make out the sound of voices.

He motioned to Ayako, who joined him. Several people were talking in a room close by. The two looked at each other.

112

What should they do? It might be foolish to attack these people; the round eyes often carried pistols. They could both be killed instantly.

Ayako pointed back to the basement door, and they retreated. They would wait a little while.

An hour passed slowly, and Ayako got up from the cold stairs and opened the basement door again. He could hear nothing, so he padded to the end of the hallway to listen. Several people were still talking in low voices, and there was an occasional chink of silverware on china. They were supping. Would they never go to bed!

Hing tiptoed up behind Ayako and nudged him, saying they ought to go on in, surprise them, and do it quickly. Ayako shook his head. They did not know how many were in the room or who they were. Also, Kelton had not supplied them with a plan of the house. They might get trapped in a room.

They were about to slip up the stairs to take care of those who might be sleeping, when they heard footsteps approach. They dashed silently for the door to the basement.

Garfield brought the four another pot of hot coffee.

Melissa said, "Please go to bed. We'll wait on ourselves if we want anything further."

"Thank you, Missy." Garfield nodded to each of them and went out quickly.

It was time for him to go, Ki said. It would be dawn in just a few hours. He stepped to the doorway and paused. Why did he feel a coldness on his cheek? It was as if a window to the outside had been opened. Yet he knew Garfield examined every window before Jessie did, making sure they were locked before he retired for the night.

Turning his head, Ki looked at Jessica. She instantly noted his changed demeanor. Something was wrong. As she continued the conversation with Melissa and Worthy, she casually adjusted her skirts and pulled her purse close, opened it and curled her fingers around the butt of the pistol inside. She smiled and laughed quietly.

Jessie caught Ki's slight nod and rose nonchalantly, strolling toward the door to the next room, where Garfield had disappeared just minutes before. There was no one in the adjoining room. She closed the door silently, glancing at Ki.

Ki stood by the door that opened on the hallway. He yanked it open suddenly. A little man clad all in black shouted, and Jessie glimpsed the steel of a knife. She drew the pistol and fired twice, watching the man—it was a coolie!—being slammed back against the wall by the force of the bullets.

Melissa screamed, and Worthy yelled as Jessica flew across the room after Ki. Ki was in the hallway, a throwing star in his hand. A second man in black ran down the hall, past the open door to the basement. He never gained the end of the hall. The *shuriken* toppled him, and he sprawled in a boneless heap on the hallway runner.

Jessie heard Worthy's voice: "What the hell happened!?"

Ki ran toward the downed man, and Jessie went back into the sitting room and knelt by the fallen Chinese. She had hit him twice in the heart. He was extremely dead.

Jessie said, "Someone sent them to kill us."

"Kelton!" Worthy said at once. "My God, what shooting! How did you know he was there?"

"I didn't. But Ki told me something was wrong."

"What do you mean, he *told* you!?" Worthy said. "He never said a thing!"

Jessica smiled. "We've worked together a long time. He didn't have to say anything."

"You two saved our lives," Melissa said breathlessly. "I don't know how you did it."

There was a banging on the front door. "Open up in there! It's the police!" came a gruff voice from outside.

Worthy stepped to the door, pulled open the large square peephole, and yelled, "Go get Inspector Jenkins! Someone just tried to kill us!" He slammed the peephole shut and heard the scurrying of footsteps and the hollering of voices.

Ki returned in another few minutes. The two Chinese had broken a window in the basement to get in, he told them. There was no one else in the house so far as he could tell. "After I go out, board up the window. I doubt if you'll have

114

any more trouble tonight. As soon as I slip out, you can let the police in."

Garfield appeared, having heard the shots. "What is it? I thought I heard shooting." He was startled, seeing the bodies. "How did these two get in?"

Jessie said, "Tell Carlos to hide, then let the police in. They'll take the bodies away."

Garfield headed for the cook's rooms.

"We'll tell them Worthy shot the one man and knifed the other." Jessie smiled. "I want to remain a foolish school friend of Melissa's. This ruse just might come in handy again soon."

Inspector Jenkins, routed from a warm bed, was grumpy and very annoyed. "There's altogether too much killing associated with this house and its occupants! Now you've got two more bodies! Who are they?"

"Assassins!" Worthy said. "They sneaked in here to kill us."

"And you killed them both?" Jenkins was impressed. "Two shots in the heart! You've got steady nerves, young man. I'll give you that."

"He's a Bancroft," Melissa said proudly.

"And you also knifed the other one in the hallway?" Jenkins regarded Worthy with new respect. "Where did you learn all that?"

"In college, Inspector."

Jenkins shook his head. What was the younger generation coming to? Did they really teach knife-throwing in college these days?

Melissa said, "I think those two coolies might have been the same ones who spooked the carriage horses, causing Father's death, Inspector."

He looked at her in astonishment. "What are you saying? There's a conspiracy against your family?"

"Of course, there is," Worthy said hotly. "Anyone in their right mind could see it! Those two were hired by someone to break in here tonight! Do you think for one minute that two Chinese would come here on their own?"

115

Jenkins stared at him. "We have absolutely no proof of anything."

"You have two bodies." Worthy could not hide his disdain.

Jenkins grunted, turning away. It *was* damn curious, he had to admit.

Melissa nodded, hands on hips as Jessica hung back.

Inspector Jenkins went outside and growled at the men who were watching the house, "Are you blind or asleep! How did those two coolies get past you!?"

It was nearly dawn by the time the coroner's wagon came and carted away the two bodies. Inspector Jenkins departed, after writing copiously in his little black notebook. Three or four newspaper reporters from the *Bulletin, Chronicle,* and *Examiner,* as well as several small local papers, pestered him, bombarding him with questions. He finally stopped long enough to make a very brief statement. He declared that several burglars had broken into the Bancroft house, nothing more. Young Worthington Bancroft, son and heir of the late W.R. Bancroft and an excellent pistol shot in his own right, had dispatched the burglars.

Jenkins went home to bed, but sleep came hard.

Chapter 15

After the coroner's men and the police had gone, no one inside the Bancroft house wanted to go to bed, although it was quite late. There had been too much excitement. Each member of the household staff wanted to be reassured. Lisa, the upstairs maid who had been attending Mrs. Bancroft, came to the head of the stairs. She wanted to know about the shots and was relieved to hear everything had been taken care of. She told Worthy and Melissa that their mother had slept through the commotion.

Mrs. Oglethorpe was on the verge of hysteria when she spotted the bloodstains on the oriental rug. Melissa calmed her down and sent her off to bed, but she returned with cleaning materials and refused to leave until the spots were removed to her satisfaction. Wet blood was easier to get up than dried blood, she insisted.

Carlos Ortega came from his hiding place in the back of the house, asking what had happened. Worthy and Jessica quickly told him what had occurred and hustled him as fast as they could back into the pantry hiding place.

Melissa said, "Carlos, please stay there for the rest of the night. The police might be back at any time."

Ki had gone; but Melissa, Worthy, and Jessica sat up, too wound-up to sleep. All they could talk about was the attack by the coolies. They felt sure they knew who had sent them.

Jessie wondered if it would be possible that Carlotta Reardon might furnish some information. Melissa and Worthy still had not deciphered parts of her diary, but they knew from what she had written that she did not love Kelton. Even so, Melissa argued, Carlotta was in the Kelton camp. Why would she put her life on the line by helping them?

Jessie explained that when she and Ki had asked Silas Dent for any information he might have on the Reardon woman, he had told them that, among other things, Carlotta was not really a "bad" woman, even though she was Kelton's mistress. There were extreme mitigating circumstances, and her story was a very sad one.

Carlotta was the daughter of one of Kelton's many gambling victims. Her father, Carlton Reardon of Philadelphia, had been a banker back in Pennsylvania and had come to California to strike it rich.

He had made a great deal of money and used it to start his own bank in San Francisco. Then he sent for his family. Unfortunately for the Reardons, Carlton had acquired the gambling bug and could not stop himself. He had finally lost everything he owned at the Kelton gaming tables. He had then committed suicide by blowing his brains out in Kelton's club. It had been one of the biggest stories of the year. Reardon's wife had wasted away, and she died soon after, leaving three children.

Two of the Reardon orphans were adopted out, being quite young, but Carlotta was a teen and was taken under Kelton's wing. He told everyone that he was taking her in out of remorse and sympathy. The courts made her his ward, and he taught her the saloon trade.

She was never a prostitute, as some suspected, but she did become an entertainer, singing and dancing with a group, which she enjoyed.

Kelton promised her marriage when she was old enough, but it never came to pass. According to Silas Dent, Carlotta grew very bitter as the years went by and her relationship with Kelton was never legitimized. Silas thought Carlotta might be willing to talk with them. Nothing ventured, nothing gained.

"She is still a young woman," said Jessie. "She has been

abused and hurt. Perhaps she would be agreeable to assisting us against the man who wronged her. It seems to me that she needs friends and attention. It might be a good idea if Ki befriended her."

The three agreed that since Carlotta had been treated so badly, she might just respond to honest affection and undemanding attention. Jessica was to ask Ki to call on her.

When Jessica saw Ki the next day, she put her idea to him, and he concurred. There was a distinct possibility he would learn something from her, and too, Carlotta was a very attractive young woman. His assignment would be more pleasure than work.

Carlotta worked at the Gold Dust Saloon every evening and night, and she seldom got home before three in the morning. Ki quickly discovered that although she was still Kelton's mistress, she was no longer living with him. She stayed in her own house instead of spending her nights with him. The only time she stayed over at Kelton's was when she acted as hostess for his social events.

It was easy for Ki to become acquainted with Carlotta at the club, since it was part of her job to meet men, to be pleasant, to induce them to stay and to gamble. She was still beautiful enough to entice men to linger a little longer instead of heading home, thus leaving more of their money at the saloon.

Carlotta found Ki to be quite attractive. His exotic good looks suggested mystery, and his manners were unusually gentle, yet not at all weak. Although they had just met, he treated her differently than the other men, and she took particular note of that at once.

She could not help being attracted to Ki. She dealt with so many men in an evening that they all seemed to blend into one rough composite. Ki was different, and the difference intrigued her. He had explained his heritage with such pride and dignity that she could not help but be impressed. He was definitely not like the others, she concluded.

She hated to say goodnight. When the club closed and she

was ready to go home, she was surprised to find Ki waiting for her by her carriage.

At first, she did not recognize him, seeing only a shadow. She dug into her purse for a derringer, preparing herself for the worst.

From the shadows, Ki spoke, "You won't need that, Miss Reardon." He stepped into the light, his hat off. "I thought I might see you safely home."

"Oh! It's you!"

"I didn't mean to alarm you."

She smiled. "I'm not alarmed anymore. You want to see me home?"

"Does that surprise you, Miss Reardon?"

"I—I suppose not, no. By the way, it's Carlotta, please call me Carlotta. Come, get in the buggy. Do you have a horse?"

"I'll tie him on behind."

Carlotta was glad to see Ki, and yet she was vaguely disappointed. He was proving to be no better than the others. All any man really wanted was her body, and obviously, Ki did, too. Why else would he meet her in a shadowy place with such a weak excuse as wanting to see her safely home?

This was not the first time she had gotten her expectations up only to have them dashed by lust.

He asked her for directions, taking up the reins. It would not do to let her know he already knew where she lived. He did not want her to be in any way suspicious of him.

They talked of the club, the only thing they knew in common. Ki had won a small amount at the tables. She told him she had been working at the Gold Dust Saloon for years, since she was quite young. She purposely avoided any mention of Kelton and wondered if Ki knew about her relationship with the saloon's owner.

When they arrived at her house, Ki drove to the stable, and the stableboy took the rig. Ki walked her to her door and politely doffed his hat.

Carlotta was astonished; he didn't push his way in. He merely wished her a pleasant night and quietly departed, a boyish smile on his exotic visage.

She had been wrong about him!

She went upstairs and undressed in a daze. In bed, she stared into the darkness, thinking about him. She had heard about gentlemen, perhaps even seen them from a distance; but in her work, she had never really met one until tonight. Kelton was anything but a gentleman, she reflected.

Carlotta found herself wanting to see Ki again.

Patrick and Terrance O'Toole were not easily inclined to forget an injustice or a hurt. They were certain they had been harmed by Josiah Kelton. One of them slightly wounded, a wound that had healed very quickly.

But quickly or not, they were not about to allow any hurt to go without answer. They wanted revenge. And they spent many nights sitting in their office drinking beer and discussing the best and most satisfying manner of avenging themselves and their family honor.

Patrick, who had been wounded, was all for using a shotgun on Kelton. Both barrels of a 12-gauge at close range should give them all the satisfaction they desired.

"It'll blow his goddamn head off!" Patrick said, relishing his idea.

"But you can't get close enough to him to do that, you idiot! He's got men around him all the time."

"Hmmm, yes, that's true. Well, what if we hit him at long range with rifles?"

Terrance nodded. "That just might work, but there's a better way."

"What?"

"Burn him out! What does Kelton like better than anything in the whole goddamn world? Money!"

"That's right!" Patrick grinned. "If we burn down the Gold Dust, we'll hurt him real bad!" He slapped his brother on the back. "Great idea, Terry! When do we do it?"

"Tomorrow, we'll go out and get us some five-gallon cans of kerosene and put 'em in the buggy. Then late at night, we can drive over there and splash the building."

They rubbed their hands together in glee and anticipation.

The following morning, Patrick sent one of their employees to buy kerosene, saying they needed it for the stoves.

Then they waited for a dark night. They did not have long to wait. When the moon was a mere sliver in the sky, when it could only be seen between patches of fog, they loaded a buggy with the kerosene, hooked up a single horse, and drove to the Gold Dust Saloon, arriving well after closing time.

The entire row of buildings was dark and silent, and the buggy wheels grated on the dirt street. They halted the rig in the alley next to the saloon and lifted down two heavy five-gallon cans. Terrance had decided that two would be enough to burn half the city. Each of them took a can.

Grady had gone to sleep in the small room behind the saloon bar. The room the bartenders used to change clothes or rest on their break; there was a cot in the corner. He woke when the last bartender nudged him.

"G'night, Grady. We're closin' up now. You gonna stay here all night?"

"Grmmuphmmf," Grady said and turned over. He yawned, thinking he really ought to get up and go home, just another minute. He closed his eyes and dropped off again. But he woke in half an hour smelling smoke.

He sat up. Smoke? *Jesus!* Fire was the constant worry of everyone. He grabbed his boots and tugged them on, then ran out of the saloon and unbolted the side door. The place was filling with smoke!

He heard flames crackling. The whole side of the building was afire! There was a single horse buggy only a dozen yards away in the alley, the horse stomping nervously.

The two O'Toole brothers ran from the carriage yard. He saw them clearly in the bright light of the burning building! They piled into the waiting buggy and drove off fast.

Grady ran for the firebell at the corner of the alley and yanked the rope madly. In minutes, he had drawn a crowd. People were yelling, some had buckets and were dousing the flames with water from the horse trough.

The fire wagon arrived, with their eccentric middle-aged socialite "mascot," Lillie Hitchcock Coit, in tow. More water was pumped while Lillie acted as a one-woman cheering section.

They fought the blaze for an hour before getting it under control, but half the building was destroyed.

Josiah Kelton arrived, swearing, running back and forth, wanting to get into the building to get his safe out, but Lillie and the firemen held him back. The second floor would not bear his weight, they told him.

Lillie tried to console Kelton, but he turned his back and a deaf ear. Walking away, he muttered to himself, "Doesn't that old dame have anything better to do than chase goddamn fire wagons?"

It took another hour before Grady dared approach him. Prepared for anything, Grady finally said, "The fire was set on purpose, boss."

Kelton rounded on him. "How do you know?"

"I seen 'em!"

Kelton grabbed the other and shook him. "Who—who did it?"

Grady shrugged. "The O'Tooles. I seen 'em both run from the side of the building and jump into a buggy."

"You're positive it was them?"

"Hell, yeh, I couldn't miss. There was plenty of light from the fire! Sure, it was them."

Kelton sighed deeply and snorted. The firemen had shown him two empty kerosene cans that had been found in the alley. So the O'Toole brothers wanted revenge, did they?

"Go get the cops," Kelton said.

The police came, and Kelton went with them to the station house and preferred charges against the O'Toole brothers for arson. He had an eyewitness.

Minutes later, the police sent men to arrest the brothers.

The building was a charred ruin, as they viewed it in daylight. The fire had burned in freaky fashion. Much of the saloon was untouched, but the gaming rooms were gutted, and Kelton's office was partially destroyed. One wall was burned, as well as part of the roof, but the safe was untouched, while many of the papers in his desk were ashes.

Kelton had men in at once to clear out the debris, which was carried away by the wagonload. Then carpenters swarmed in and began to put the building back together again.

One curious incident happened to Grady the night of the fire. An incident he had not told to Kelton, fearing his wrath. Grady had seen a man laughing as the flames bit into the Gold Dust building.

"What's so damn funny?" Grady had demanded.

The man only shook his head and limped away.

His building would take months to restore, and Kelton brooded over it. There was no way to rebuild it faster. The men were doing all they could as fast as they could.

But there was a way to put himself back into the casino business quicker than that. Kelton held a number of mortgages. And one of them was due immediately, Bert Hutchinson's. He had told Bert that he would renew, but this was an emergency. He sent Bert a note telling him that he needed the store and would foreclose if Bert could not pay up instantly. He was sure Bert would not be able to raise the amount needed in time.

Bert owned a large dry-goods store, and Kelton figured with certain alterations and much decorating, it would do as a gambling casino. The location was even better than the Gold Dust.

Kelton was in good spirits. When he saw Carlotta, he said, "Tonight we celebrate!"

She looked at him blankly. "Celebrate what? The burned-out building?"

"The fire was not all bad, my dear. Now I will have two casinos. Between them, we will corral all the bettors in the area. I'll import crystal chandeliers, floor-to-ceiling mirrors from Europe, the finest carpets and paintings. It'll be the grandest gambling house in the West. I think I'll call the new one the Kelton Palace. Do you like the sound of it?"

She shrugged. "It makes no difference to me."

"You could show a little more interest!"

"Why should I?"

He blew out his breath. "You're impossible!"

"*I'm* impossible!? You tell me about your mahogany tables

124

and gilt ceilings and expect me to get excited over them? Why? I'm just an employee."

"You're more than that, and you know it!"

"Oh, am I?" She held out her left hand and waggled her ring finger. "Do you see a ring there? A *promised* ring?"

He snorted and stalked away. *What a harridan! What an ungrateful bitch!*

Bert Hutchinson sent a note to Worthy Bancroft. *Must see you as soon as possible. May I come to the house this afternoon?*

Worthy sent a reply by the same messenger. *By all means. Come at your convenience.*

After the messenger left, Worthy discussed Bert's note with Melissa. "I wonder what he wants," he said, puzzled.

By chance, Garfield was in the room. "With your permission, sir, may I venture a guess?"

They turned to look at the butler.

"Of course. What?"

Garfield cleared his throat dramatically. "The gossip is, sir, that Councilman Hutchinson has been foreclosed on by that Kelton person."

"How have you heard this?" Worthy was astonished.

"The markets are a sea of gossip, sir. Everything that happens in The City is discussed there. I heard that story this morning from three different mouths."

"Good heavens!" Melissa said. "Is nothing sacred?"

"Very little, Missy," Garfield replied.

Worthy paced the room. "So he wants money."

Garfield persisted. "But according to what I have heard, sir, it is already too late for that."

"Hutchinson has lost the store he owned?"

"I'm afraid so, sir."

★

Chapter 16

Ki arrived at Carlotta's doorstep right on time. After complimenting her on her violet organdy afternoon dress, with matching parasol and white lace petticoats, he escorted her to the waiting carriage. He appreciatively took in the loveliness of her dark hair and eyes and her ivory complexion; she was quite stunning.

They drove at once to Tadich's and were shown to a reserved table. She looked around in delight. "I have never been here before."

"Then it's high time."

She glanced around the room self-consciously. "I think they're staring at us."

Ki shook his head. "They're staring at *you*. Don't notice them. Possibly none of them have seen a beautiful woman before, and you are the loveliest woman here."

"Ki, do you mean that!?"

"Certainly," he said in all honesty. "Now, would you like some wine?"

Her dark eyes widened. "Wine with lunch?"

Smiling, he said, "Why not?" He beckoned the wine steward, who rushed to the table.

They were eating their lobster when Ki noticed the man in the gaudy bemedaled uniform who had just entered, accompanied by two scruffy-looking dogs. "Who in the world is that?"

It was Carlotta's turn to smile. "That's Emperor Norton!"

"Emperor!?"

She laughed. "Yes, emperor. He is the self-proclaimed Norton the First, Emperor of the United States and Protector of Mexico. The mutts are Bummer and Lazarus, strays that are his constant companions. Believe it or not, San Franciscans love him! He actually believes he *is* emperor, and we go along with him. In fact, the city council voted him thirty dollars a year for uniforms, and his own currency is printed for him and accepted everywhere. He and the royal dogs have their own seats at the theatre, and a railroad and a steamship line have issued him lifetime passes with dining privileges."

Ki was astonished. He watched as Emperor Norton and his dogs were shown to a fine table. Waiters hovered over him as if he really were royalty instead of the penniless town eccentric. Everyone treated him with the utmost respect.

"Amazing!"

"He's harmless," Carlotta said, "And he gives The City a certain air, don't you think?"

"I think it could only happen in San Francisco!"

When they left the restaurant, she held his arm. Looking up at him, she said wistfully, "I've had a wonderful time. I really don't want to go back to the club tonight, but I must."

They drove to her house, and he walked her to the door again. This time, he kissed her hand before departing.

Carlotta gazed after him and sighed. As she went inside, she looked at the back of her hand. No one had ever done that before.

Jessie met Ki at the Nugget Hotel, and they went together to see Silas Dent. He was sitting in his office, his coat off, his hawk face looking pleased to see Jessica.

Jessie wasted no time in getting to the point of their visit. "Silas, we hear that Kelton has foreclosed on some property here in The City."

"Yes, that's right," Dent said. "Councilman Hutchinson's store. Kelton plans to make a casino out of it."

She asked, "What's the talk? Will Kelton rebuild the Gold Dust?"

"Sure, probably."

"Then he'll have the lion's share of gambling in The City," Ki said frowning.

"Well," Silas said, scratching his chin, "Kelton holds IOUs on just about everyone in town—not me, of course—and holds mortgages on the rest. He's become a real financial mogul. He controls two banks, you know. Gambling has paid off for him in a big way." Silas opened a humidor, took out a large cigar, and rolled it between his fingers. "I don't think many people know about the banks."

Jessie clucked her tongue. "How can such a crook fool so many people?"

"I'm not so sure he fools them. But facts are facts. He *does* own a great deal of property, much of which he bought when it was dirt cheap." Silas lit the cigar, puffing luxuriously. "Also, he's into politics. It's common knowledge that he owns several politicians. You must have heard that already."

Jessie nodded.

"And the inside talk is that he's being blackmailed by one of them, a very high official."

Ki smiled. "Now that's interesting."

"Yes indeed. From what I hear, this person wants his IOUs back and money on top of it." Silas shrugged and blew a large smoke ring. "However, I don't know who that official is, and I wouldn't care to speculate."

Jessie mused, "I wonder if the blackmail has anything to do with W.R. Bancroft's death."

When the pair left Silas Dent's office, Jessie wanted to see how the work was progressing on Kelton's fire-damaged building. They grabbed the nearest hack and drove there to look, pulling up opposite the site.

The saloon was open and operating as usual; but there was a board fence around the rest of the building, and workmen were swarming over the construction area. The near-deafening sound of saws and hammers was continuous.

They asked the cabbie to wait and got out. Ki stopped one of the workmen and asked about Kelton's offices.

"They all been moved to the new place," the man told them

curiously. He fixed Ki with a quizzical look. "Funny, you the second t'ask about that today."

"Who else asked?" Jessica asked, moving closer to the workman so she could hear better.

The man looked her over and took a long breath. "Feller in a cape, old codger. Had a limp."

Jessica fluttered her lashes at him. "Thank you."

They walked back to the hack. "Hmmm, the mystery man," Ki said. "I wonder what he wants with Kelton?"

Ki had not intended a love affair with Carlotta, but the situation was getting a bit out of hand. He *was* attracted to her, and she appeared to be equally drawn to him. This was undeniable.

For the time being, Carlotta was not working in the saloon. Kelton had wanted her to circulate among the men on the floor, she told Ki, and get them to buy her drinks. But she had refused, turning Kelton down flat and telling him she was an entertainer, not a bar girl.

"If Josiah won't let me entertain on the stage," she said, pouting, "then I will just leave the club. I can always go somewhere else. There are plenty of clubs in town that'd hire me in a second." She plumped her sofa cushion and inched closer to Ki.

He frowned and said, "Doesn't Kelton control enough of the town so he could have you barred from all the other clubs if he wanted to?"

Carlotta sighed deeply and glanced around her parlor. "Yes, more than likely. But there are other towns, you know. There are stages running out of San Francisco every day."

Because she knew Ki was coming over, Carlotta had sent her housekeeper on enough errands to keep her away most of the day. She moved even closer to Ki and slid her arms about his neck. "If I left town, would you miss me?"

"The entire city would miss you."

She threw her head back and laughed daintily. "You always say the right things. How is it that some woman hasn't hog-tied you before this?"

"I'm very hard to catch." He took her in his arms and

kissed her fully, then sat back for a moment. "Why haven't *you* married Kelton long ago?"

Carlotta's face changed as she moved away, her back stiffening. "I hate him! I would never marry him! He promised me marriage ages ago, then put it off and put it off until I finally realized he had lied to me from the very beginning. He never intended to marry me! He considers me his property!" Her dark eyes flashed as she spat out the words. "His property! Like his horse or his saloon or that house of his with the lake inside it."

"Lake?" Ki said, genuinely surprised and quite puzzled. "A lake inside a house?"

"Well," she said, calming down slightly, "a pond, at least. It's where he keeps his safe."

"Incredible!" Ki said, staring at her in near-disbelief. "He keeps a safe underwater?"

She smirked. "It's the safest place in town. Of course, it's a secret even from me. He doesn't know I found out about it. He got the idea from Mark Hopkins, who had a private reservoir sunk into his Nob Hill front courtyard for use just in case of fire."

"I see," Ki said, trying not to appear too anxious. "So Kelton lowers a safe into his private inside pond, does he? I guess he must have some very important papers to keep in something as complicated as that." He tried to remain as casual and conversational as possible.

She nodded earnestly, "Yes, all his mortgages and deeds and IOUs, plus tons of money and secret papers. He keeps small amounts of money in the safe in his office at the Gold Dust, but that's all. All the really important stuff is in the pond." She laughed at what she considered a joke.

Ki smiled to himself as he chuckled along with her. *Then we didn't lose anything by not being able to get into that office safe.* He said, "And I bet he keeps a permanent lifeguard on that pond of his, right?"

She laughed long before answering. "No, of course not, silly. I told you. It's a secret." She sobered for a moment and said proudly, "No one's supposed to know it's there. I only discovered it by accident. The pond is in a locked area of the basement. When Kelton wants to get something from it, he locks himself in. I followed him one night when we were alone in the house." Her smile broadened. "He thought I was asleep, so he didn't bother locking the door behind him when he went in." She laughed, obviously pleased with herself. "I saw him raise the safe and open it."

"Very interesting." Ki got up and walked across the room. He stood gazing out the window at the city.

She followed him, hugging him from behind and leaning her head on his broad back. "If you're thinking of getting into that safe," she whispered, "it's impossible."

His body went imperceptibly rigid, then relaxed. He turned and kissed her. "Is it?"

She took a breath and stared deep into his eyes. "If I thought you could, I'd help you any way I could. But I know it is impossible."

Ki kissed her again, passionately. Brushing a lock of her dark hair aside, he said, "I've done several things that were considered impossible. Let me think about this."

It was late when Ki left Carlotta and rode to the Bancroft mansion. As always, he left his horse in the copse of trees some distance from the house and snaked his way to the basement past the police guards and a couple of Kelton's men.

Melissa was already in bed, but she got up at once when Jessie came into her room.

"Ki's here," Jessie announced, "and he's got some news for us."

Melissa knocked on Worthy's door, and the four gathered in the small sitting room. Ki told them what he had learned from Carlotta. Kelton kept an underwater safe in his fortress of a house.

"Then it's impossible," Melissa said, shaking her head and looking from Ki to Jessie. "We'll never find out what he had on Daddy."

Worthy asked Ki, "What do you think? Is it really all that impossible?"

Ki smiled wisely. "According to the old saying, nothing is

131

impossible." He winked at Jessie. "Well, nothing within reason."

"A diversion," Worthy said excitedly. "Divert his attention."

"My thoughts exactly," Ki agreed. "I think a diversion is the only answer. But it'll be tricky. Kelton's no fool." He cocked his head and looked toward the front of the house. "What's that noise outside?"

Melissa ran in the direction of the noise. "Oh, my! It's the police! There's well over a dozen of them on the walk out front!"

Worthy said instantly, "They're planning to search the house again! Ki, get into the secret room with Carlos! Melissa, keep them out for a minute or two! Wait for Garfield to answer the door, and then stall them!"

The police search turned up nothing again. Inspector Jenkins was there, chewing on a cheap cigar and looking very pained by the ordeal.

Melissa said acidly, "This is disgraceful, Inspector, getting honest people out of bed at this hour of the night! If my father were alive, he'd have you walking a beat by morning!"

"No disrespect, Miss Bancroft, but if your father were alive, I wouldn't have to do this," Jenkins said stiffly. "I'm just doing my duty. We suspect you and your brother of harboring Carlos Ortega."

"Well, if we're hiding him, then why can't you and your men find him!"

Jenkins made a growling sound somewhere deep in his throat. "Sooner or later." He openly frowned at her.

Garfield held the front door open formally as Melissa demanded, "When are you going to get those big-footed policemen out of my house?" She glared at the inspector defiantly.

"Very well." Jenkins motioned to a sergeant, and the police filed out. Jenkins followed them, pausing at the front door. "Sooner or later, young lady," he threatened, grabbing the door from Garfield and slamming it behind him.

Melissa fell into a chair. "Garfield, please bolt the door on your way to bed."

Ki came out of the secret room. Carlos, he told them, had slept through the raid. "Thank goodness he doesn't snore," he said, only half-joking.

Everyone laughed, releasing a little of their pent-up tensions.

"From what I could hear," Ki said when they had finished chuckling, "that inspector is near the breaking point. He means business."

Jessie nodded. "Yes, you're right. Perhaps we can be a little less hard on him. After all, as he said, he is only doing his duty."

Worthy and Melissa looked at her with near-belligerence, and Worthy opened his mouth to speak, only to be cut off.

"Excuse me," Ki said abruptly, "but while I was in that hole, in the dark, I thought of something."

Worthy, his train of thought sidetracked, said, "What?"

"We were talking about a diversion, remember? Well, I've been thinking about it. I think the O'Tooles just might be interested in helping us. They hate Kelton, don't they? Why not ask them to join us."

Worthy clapped Ki on the back. "That is a great idea!"

Melissa applauded in assent.

"But they're still in jail," Jessie pointed out.

"We can get them out on bail,"—Worthy snapped his fingers—"just like that. I'll go see Bert Hutchinson. He hates Kelton, too, and he's our lawyer. He'll help us."

Melissa smiled. "I think he will, too."

Chapter 17

Ki was urged to stay in the house that night, but his horse was tied in the copse of trees, so he did not. The others went to bed at once.

Worthy sat up in his room, trying to keep his mind on the plan, the O'Toole brothers, and how to get at the safe in the pool, but his thoughts kept sliding away. To Jessie. She was the most appealing creature he had ever known, and it was difficult for him to stay in the same house with her without wanting to be with her.

Undressing, he put on a robe over his pajama bottoms and went out to the dark hallway, pausing by her door. He raised his hand to knock and stopped. What if she should turn a cold shoulder to him this time? Usually so sure of himself, he now had doubts.

He returned to his room and leaned against the door. *What was that old adage? Nothing ventured, nothing gained?* He wondered if that applied to beautiful women. Their first time together had been unbelievable, but she had been all business afterward, at least, in public.

Worthy went back to her door, turned the knob silently, and opened it several inches. By the light of the full moon streaming in through the window, he could see her in bed. Was she asleep? He eased inside and closed the door behind him. Then he padded to the bed, and as he reached it, she sat up, a revolver in her hand. He heard the *click-clack* as she pulled back the hammer.

Then she obviously recognized him in the moonlight's gloom. "Oh, it's you!"

Worthy was rigid, staring at the pistol. This woman was a true tigress. Had he thought that before? As his eyes became accustomed to the dark, he saw her put the gun away and smile up at him.

"Reflex action," she said lightly, patting the side of the bed. "Come and sit down."

He sat and took her hand in his. It was soft and supple and gave no hint of the things it could do with a revolver. He wondered all at once if anyone would ever tame this lovely creature. He doubted it. She might allow herself to be tamed for the moment, if she pleased, but . . .

She said, "I hoped you would come back." Her voice was husky with promise.

He stared at her, removed his robe and pajama bottoms, then leaned forward to kiss her. She returned his kiss and pulled at him. He slid into bed with her, his body ready for the pleasure only his tigress could deliver.

She was naked, and her legs wrapped around his hips, pulling him to her. Before he could move, she pushed him down on his back and swung up on top. As he lay there, watching her full breasts heave and her pink nipples stiffen with excitement, she teased his erect manhood with the moist warmth of her womanhood. On her knees, she lowered herself just enough to swallow the sensitive head into her hot wetness, then pulled up, laughing.

He took her firm breasts in both hands and squeezed gently, then more urgently, pulling her down to him. Her mouth reached for his. Tongues and lips blended, but she kept her hips up, teasing, taunting. Down, she dipped, then up again, then down a little farther. When Worthy was sure he couldn't stand another minute of this sublime torture, she thrust herself all the way down, plunging his throbbing erection deep inside her to the rubbery wall.

Worthy gasped and cried out, deaf to her nearly identical cry. She twisted her hips slowly at first, then faster, and ground herself into his crotch, twisting and turning, flexing muscles within that grabbed hold of his member and tugged wildly at it. His fingers dug into the flesh of her perfect breasts, her rigid nipples pulsating in his palms.

As she rode him frantically, squeezing him from the inside, he reached a free hand into her moistness and searched for her nub of pleasure. Large and hot, it met his hand and sent tingles of excitement through him.

"Yes! Oh, yes!" she cried.

Worthy's fingers and thumb pinched the erotic nubbin and pulled on it hard. She screamed with delight. His other hand twisted and pulled on her nipple. Rolling the two delicious female erections between his fingers, he saw the grimace of painful pleasure on her lovely face. Beads of perspiration ran down her face and chest, and her long blonde curls clung to her face and body.

"Oh, my God!" he yelled, as his erection cried out for release. His body stiffened, and his back raised off the bed in at attempt to thrust himself even deeper. He nearly lifted her off the bed.

Relaxing her inner muscles, she slowed her pace down and purposely kept him from reaching his peak. She whispered and stroked his tiny hard nipples and kissed his lips. Her tongue circled his mouth, tingling his lips. She felt him relax a little, although his erection was still full.

Just as he felt awash with peace and pleasure, she bit into his lip and sucked as hard as she could. He felt his member engorge with sudden passion as her hips began to swing again and her muscles clamped down and tightened inside.

Every time he came close enough to release, she slowed the process down and waited for him to relax, then up and away again. The tension built to the breaking point, and he pleaded with her for more, no more, more, no more.

With one last thrust, he cried out, "You gorgeous cat!" and lit up the skies within his head.

She threw back her head and a howl of delight poured forth as her body shook orgasmically. Her inner muscles throbbed and convulsed and wrung his manhood dry.

She dropped to his chest, limp and submissive, her profuse

perspiration pooling with his. Two sweat-soaked bodies pulsed as one while the lovers paused to catch their breath.

Worthy knew this would be a night to remember if he lived through Jessie's animal passion.

Melissa paced the floor of the huge parlor, feeling a restlessness she had not experienced for ages. She had been cooped up in the house forever! It was unnatural! Besides, the sun was shining brightly outside, which was not all that usual in The City shrouded with fog. The world appeared very peaceful out there. She made up her mind and went to find Jessie.

"Jessie, I simply cannot stay in this house another minute! I must get out or I'll go mad!"

Jessie gazed at her sympathetically. She and Worthy had already relieved their tensions, but Missy . . . She smiled and said, "I understand."

"Then let's go! I know. Let's go shopping!"

"Missy, you know it's dangerous. I'm sure Kelton would have you killed on sight."

"At this point, I don't care! I'd rather be dead outside than cooped up in here forever!" She sighed forlornly. "Oh, I don't mean that."

"I know," Jessie said with understanding. "I think I would feel the same way if I were you. Come on, Missy, get dressed and we'll go out." She smiled broadly as Melissa's sad face suddenly lit up.

Jessie dressed carefully. She examined her pistol and put it into her purse. She tucked a derringer into her silken sash, took a parasol with a sharp point, and went downstairs to find Garfield.

"Send a messenger to Ki at the Nugget. Ask him to meet us at the St. Francis. It's very important."

"Yes, Miss Jessie. At once."

"Thank you. Not a word to Missy."

Garfield nodded and had the carriage brought around, and the two young women were off.

Melissa was like a young girl again. "Let's have lunch at some nice place first, shall we? Can we?"

"How about the St. Francis?" Jessie said as if just thinking of it.

"Marvelous!" Melissa clapped her hands with delight. "There are ever so many shops near there."

"What did you want to shop for?"

"Oh, I thought maybe a fur. It'll be winter before we know it, as much winter as The City ever gets. And perhaps some rings."

Jessie smiled. She herself had little chance to wear beautiful jewelry, and she could never bring herself to wear an animal that had been trapped. But it was fun for a change to look in the stores and to be feminine, if only for a little while.

A liveried boy let down the buggy's steps for them and held the door of the carriage as they stepped out at the St. Francis Hotel.

Melissa asked the driver to wait for them, and he lifted his hat. "Yes, miss."

Without seeming to, Jessie surveyed the street and the crowd, her sharp eye missing very little. Was there a sudden movement in a doorway? Did someone duck out of sight as her head turned?

She said nothing to Melissa, and they entered the hotel. The "someone" Jessie had spotted wore a derby hat, not an unusual headpiece, and she might have been wrong. But she didn't think so. If someone had recognized them, would he notify Kelton? He just might.

Jessie also kept her eyes moving for the welcome sight of Ki. She finally caught a glimpse of him while Melissa greeted a friend and chatted for a moment. After saying hello, Jessie excused herself and moved to the kiosk, pretending to look for a particular newspaper.

Ki approached. "Why is Melissa here?"

"She simply would not stay inside another moment. She was becoming upset, and I feared she might do something rash if I didn't pacify her with this little trip."

He let out his breath. "I don't like it at all!"

Jessie saw that Melissa was finishing her chat. She had only time to tell Ki to "watch for a man in a derby hat" before

138

returning to say goodbye to the friend. Then she led Melissa into the restaurant.

The maitre d' escorted them to a table near the terrace, and Melissa was like a child in her delight. She was out in the world again, among people! How could danger touch her here? She beamed with joy and prattled on.

Jessie used the large menu the waiter presented her to survey the tables. Derby Hat was not in evidence. Of course, he would not wear his hat inside, and she had not gotten a very good look at his face other than that he was clean-shaven. But no one evinced any particular interest in them outside of the usual appreciative glances.

Jessie allowed herself a tiny glass of wine; then they ordered. She decided on brook trout poached in butter; Melissa ordered sea bass with capers. Melissa's eyes followed each course as it came. She was enjoying herself completely.

The young women talked of everything but their troubles as they ate. Jessie could see Ki at the far end of the room; he came and went, keeping an eye on them.

When they finished lunch, they left the room casually, drawing dozens of eyes to them. Jessie was amused at the looks, merely a matter of clothes. Other women would not look at her twice if she were in her jeans and man's shirt.

As they reached the street, Melissa pointed to a shop not far off, saying she wanted to go into it.

Jessie said, "It's very near an unsavory section. Do you think it's wise? It's too close to Morton Street."

"Oh, Jessie, look at the sun! It's a beautiful, serene day, and besides, no one knows we're here."

That might not be exactly true, Jessie thought, but she had not seen Derby Hat since that first quick glimpse. And, of course, Ki was nearby.

"Come on," Melissa said, taking her arm and tugging. "We can walk it in a couple of minutes."

Reluctantly, Jessie followed along, allowing her young friend to lead the way. She pulled her purse around and opened it so she would have no problems if she needed to plunge her hand inside.

• • •

Ki followed the two young women at a small distance, his eyes everywhere. And it was with no shock that he recognized Kelton's man, Zack. Obviously, Zack must have been watching the Bancroft house and followed the two women here. With Zack was a lean man wearing a derby hat. So Jessie had been right!

Ki edged closer to the two men, who were separating to approach the two women, one from each side. He gave a little shrill whistle that Jessie would recognize as a danger signal. As Derby Hat slipped a knife from his belt, Ki darted in and leaped into a *tobi-geri* kick as he gave a quick yell. The man turned his head slightly, and Ki's foot smashed into the man's Adam's apple. Derby Hat toppled, and his knife clattered away in the crowd.

Several people yelped, looking at the threshing man on the ground. Jessie's revolver, held close to her body, fired at Zack as she whirled toward him. Zack's eyes opened wide in surprise as the slug doubled him up. He stumbled and went to his knees. His mouth opened to yell, but nothing came out.

Jessie grabbed Melissa's arm and hurried her into the nearest store. Ki joined them in another moment, as people gathered about the two fallen men on the walkway. Someone was shouting for the police.

Ki said urgently, "You must not stay here. Come with me." He led them to the back of the store, ignoring the salesman's simpering protests.

They went through the rear door, into an alley, and out to the side street. Ki faced them then, saying, "No more of this foolishness." He lectured Melissa. "You are in extreme danger. Go home and stay there!"

Melissa pouted sheepishly. "I only thought—"

"It's my fault," Jessie said earnestly. "Put *me* over your knee."

Ki rolled his eyes, stepped into the street, and hailed the Bancroft carriage, which was just at the corner. He saw them into it and then hailed a hack for himself. He had the driver follow the carriage back to the Bancroft house and watched until the two young women were safely inside.

Chapter 18

Josiah Kelton was furious. A messenger had brought him the news. Zack and Freddie Waters, who had both been watching the Bancroft house, had followed Melissa Bancroft and the gorgeous blonde woman and planned to dispatch them. When the two men had closed in for the kill, a mysterious passerby had killed both of them!

Kelton raged, "Who was it? Who killed them?"

The messenger had no idea. He had told all he knew.

Kelton sent him to the police station with a note to Sergeant LaPine. In an hour, LaPine came to Kelton's office.

"We don't know who killed the two men. One was shot at close range, and the other's neck was broken. He was hit in the throat very hard, all the bones smashed."

"Could the women have done it?"

"No, certainly not." LaPine shook his head. "It took great strength. We have a few witnesses, who all contradict one another." He sighed. "But several agree that a mysterious stranger killed Waters, and someone else shot Zack. Nobody is quite sure where the shot came from. It all happened very fast."

"What happened to the two women?"

"They disappeared while everyone was milling about."

Kelton offered the sergeant a cigar and said, "It's very disturbing. A citizen cannot walk on the streets without getting shot! Where were the bodies taken?"

"To the Rockey Mortuary. Are you going to pay for the funerals?"

"I'll take up a collection," Kelton said. "They worked for me, doing odd jobs."

When the sergeant was gone, Kelton sat looking out the window. He could offer a reward for information. Maybe a witness would come forward.

He made up his mind and went to his desk to draw up a poster. When he had it worded to his satisfaction, he called in a hanger-on, Eddie Botts, and told him to take it to the nearest printer to have one hundred copies made.

"Then have them tacked up all over town, especially around the St. Francis."

Botts nodded and hurried out.

Conrad Hutchinson, a calf look on his sallow face, appeared at the Bancroft mansion with a message for Worthy.

Worthy came downstairs at once. "Hello, Conrad, you're a messenger now?"

"Well," he said hesitantly, "I . . . offered to bring this letter."

He looked around for Jessie as Worthy read the note. It was from Bert. Worthy read it with mounting excitement. Bert had been contacted by Archie Weaver! Weaver wanted to meet with the Bancrofts. Could Worthy and Melissa please come to Bert's office?

Worthy folded the note. "Tell your father I'll give him an answer later today."

Conrad looked disappointed. Worthy took him to the door and watched him shamble down the steps to the street. Then he went to show the note to Melissa and Jessie.

"Could it be a trap?" Jessie asked.

"Hutchinson is a councilman, our attorney and a friend," Melissa replied. "He wouldn't set a trap for us."

"Nevertheless, I think Weaver should come here. It's too dangerous to go out where Kelton's men can catch either of you in the open as they did yesterday."

"That's true," Worthy said, nodding. "All right, I'll send word that if he wants to talk to us, he must come here."

Melissa bit her lip. "Is it possible that we'll solve the whole mystery! Archie Weaver must have quite a tale to tell!"

"He wants money," Worthy said. "Father must have been supporting him."

"Then we'll give him money," Melissa said emphatically.

Worthy got up to send the message. "I'll tell him to come at ten tomorrow morning."

The next morning, there was much anticipation in the Bancroft household. The mysterious Archie Weaver was about to appear! As ten o'clock approached, Worthy paced the room, and Melissa cried out. A half-dozen policemen were gathering in front of the house.

Worthy yelled, "It's another of their damn raids! They've come to search the house again!"

Melissa dashed from the kitchen, shouting for Carlos to hide.

There was a loud pounding on the front door, and Inspector Jenkins's voice called out, "Open up, open up!"

Garfield strode to the door and flung it open, disdainfully.

Worthy, lounging near the entrance, said, "What is it this time, Inspector?"

Jenkins had another search warrant and strode past, giving orders sharply. The bluecoats scattered as Melissa ran upstairs to guard her mother's privacy.

Jessie wandered out the front door, ignoring the appreciative looks of the policemen, and stood for a moment on the porch as if taking the air. She was watching for Archie Weaver, but she did not see him. Undoubtedly, he had seen the police and had hidden himself. She went back inside. Catching Worthy's eye, she shook her head in a tiny gesture.

Jenkins's men found nothing.

Melissa said acidly, "I'm sure we should all be proud to live in a land where the police search our houses continually!"

"Ma'am, you are under suspicion."

"And you, sir, are beneath contempt!"

Archie Weaver spotted the police assembling in front of the Bancroft house and withdrew. In another moment, he would have been climbing the front steps.

He waited, some distance away, till the crowd of bluecoats

left. But several of their number stayed to patrol the vicinity. Had this been a trap? Had the Bancrofts planned to have him arrested? He hurried back to Bert Hutchinson's office, and Bert explained the police searches. They agreed that it was too risky to meet at the Bancroft house.

Bert wrote Worthy another note.

Melissa read the note Worthy handed her and passed it to Jessie. In Bert Hutchinson's own hand, it read: "There are private police to be hired if you feel the need to be accompanied here."

Jessie said, "Ki and I will go with you. Archie is probably very nervous. He may also fear for his life."

They sent the messenger back with two notes, one for Ki and one for Hutchinson, saying they would be in his office that afternoon.

Ki arrived at Hutchinson's office just as Worthy, Melissa, and Jessie's carriage drew up out front. They had all gotten there without incident. Archie Weaver was waiting for them.

He was an old man with a lined, weathered face; a lean body, stooped with age; thick gray brows; and gnarled hands. As he stepped forward to greet them, he walked with a definite limp. His clothes were old and stained, but his eyes were bright as a bird's as they danced from one to the other during introductions.

Bert Hutchinson brought them all into his private office and warned his secretary that he was not to be disturbed.

"Archie has a lot to tell you," Hutchinson said, seating himself behind his massive desk. "Archie, you have the floor."

Archie nodded solemnly. "Well, let me start a long time back then." He glanced at Melissa. "When you were just a tot. Your daddy and I were partners in several mines. We were digging for gold in those days, and we had a few good strikes. Enough to buy beans with and put a little by for a rainy day."

Worthy asked, "There were only two of you?"

"Yes, at first. Just me and W.R. Then a few years later, after we brought our families out, we took another partner, Homer Kelsey." Archie paused to sip the coffee Bert had put by his elbow. "Homer seemed like a good feller at first. He convinced us we needed him, so we took him in rather than hire someone to help us with the work, and there was plenty.

"Homer turned out to be a slick talker, and on the nights when we sat around the fire, he started talking about the future. What were we gonna do with the money we were piling up? Gold dust and silver ore and money were the same things in them days. What he wanted us to do was form a tontine. And we finally did."

Melissa asked, "What's a tontine?"

Archie looked at Hutchinson, who said, "It's a legal document, a form of life annuity. The individual profits increase as the number of survivors diminishes."

Jessie said in surprise, "You mean, winner takes all?"

"Survivor takes all, yes."

The room fell silent a moment as the four took this in.

Melissa finally broke the silence. "Survivor takes all! And this was Kelsey's idea?"

"Yes, it was," Weaver answered. "W.R. and I really didn't like the idea much, what with our families and all, but Kelsey was, as I said, a slick talker. We finally put our signatures on the paper, and I have regretted it ever since."

Hutchinson remarked, "Archie thinks Kelsey burned down his house. He lost his family in the fire and was almost killed himself."

"M'leg was crushed by a falling timber." Archie tapped his wooden leg. "I don't know how I got out of there or how Kelsey didn't spot me. But I did. Some friends got me to a doc—"

"No one knew he was alive," Hutchinson said, "and he kept it that way."

"Until I saw Bancroft again. He gave me money to live on. I was searching for Kelsey. I wanted revenge for all the misery he brought down on me."

Worthy asked, "Did you find him?"

Archie nodded. "Right here in San Francisco. He calls hisself Josiah Kelton now. He took my share of what we put by, and it was a lot. Him and W.R. split up, of course. After the fire, W.R. wouldn't have nothing to do with Kelsey. He couldn't prove nothing against him, but he didn't trust him."

"Why didn't you go to the law?" Melissa asked.

"I did, but nobody would believe me. I had lost everything I owned in that fire and couldn't prove a thing. It took me a long time to recover from the fire, to get this here leg attached and all. By then, I didn't even know where to find W.R. It took me years. I didn't know he'd come right here. I heard he'd gone back East with his family and was living there."

Melissa said, "Worthy and I went to school in the East."

Hutchinson added, "So Kelsey, or Kelton, stole Archie's share of the profits and started up his own business here. Now what's Kelton's is half Archie's."

Archie said sourly, "He'd kill you for sayin' that."

Melissa asked, "So what did you do when you finally found my father?"

"I went to him and we talked. He had already built your big house on the hill." Archie grinned. "At first, he didn't believe I was alive. He thought I went up in the fire. Then he asked me what I needed, and I told him. He give me money to live on." He smiled wryly. "I got to admit, I was worried that he and Kelsey were in cahoots to get my share. But then I realized that W.R. would never do nothing so vicious."

"But there was something else," the councilman prompted. "Tell them, Archie."

The old man nodded. "W.R. was bein' blackmailed by Kelsey. I mean, Kelton. Kelton never married, and he built that fort he lives in. But W.R. had his missus and you two."

Worthy was astounded. "Our father blackmailed? Why?"

"Because of you two and your mother. Kelton told W.R. that something terrible'd happen to his family one by one if W.R. didn't pay him five thousand a week." Archie looked from one to the other. "I told you, Kelton's a vicious man!"

In a small voice, Melissa asked, "And did Daddy pay it?"

"Well, sure. By this time, he knew what kind of varmint Kelton was. He told me it was better for him to pay than take a chance that Kelton might really kill one of you. 'Course, there was a time when W.R. would have done something else, but now he was soft and getting older, like me. We were both older than Kelton, and he wanted to live peaceably."

Jessie murmured, "But W.R. was killed."

146

"Yes, and he feared that might happen. Kelton held the tontine; remember, survivor takes all." He looked at them. "Now Kelton has only t'kill me."

Melissa said, "But why would Kelton kill Worthy and me? Because we're the Bancroft heirs?"

"Yes, of course," said Hutchinson. "With you two dead, he can take over all the Bancroft holdings. The tontine says so." The attorney fiddled with a cigar. "I want Archie to leave The City. Go somewhere he'll be safe until this affair is settled." He rattled a sheet of paper. "I have Archie's copy of the tontine here. It will be kept safe." Bert looked at Worthy. "Do you know where your father's copy is?"

Worthy looked at Melissa, then shook his head. "I didn't know about it, so I never looked for it."

"Me, either," Melissa said, glancing from one to the other. "We'll search his papers."

"Good." Hutchinson nodded. "Archie doesn't think Kelton knows he's still alive, so one day it will come as a shock to him when we're ready to move against him legally. However, in order to do that, we need a good case of proof. We *suspect* Kelton of a lot of things. We must prove them when we get to court."

Melissa thought immediately of Carlotta's diary. *If* they could decipher it, it might tell them a good deal. And *if* she herself would testify in their behalf.

Worthy asked, "Not to change the subject, but why did Father and Mother go to Kelton's dinner that night?"

The attorney said, "In my opinion, your father went there to try to get Kelton to tear up the tontine. He also wanted Kelton to stop bleeding him." Hutchinson glanced from Melissa to Worthy. "Has Kelton asked you two for money since your father's death?"

"No, of course not," said Worthy in disgust. "And if he does—"

"Well, the next thing," Jessie interrupted in a businesslike tone, "is to make sure Mr. Weaver is safe." She turned to Archie. "Where do you think you would like to go?"

Archie had a ready answer; he had evidently been thinking about it. "Rio Bonito," he said. "It's a little settlement up on the Russian River. Kelton won't never find me there."

"All right, then that's where you should go."

"We'll arrange it," Worthy agreed. "How soon can you leave, Mr. Weaver?"

The old man shrugged. "Ever'thing I own in the world is in this room with me. I kin go right now, iffen you like."

"Good," Hutchinson said. "Then you stay in this office till dark. We'll get you a ticket on the northbound stage. Is there a telegraph in Rio Bonito?"

"Nope, but a letter to the postmaster addressed to me should reach me."

"I'll see you off on the stage," Ki said.

"And I'll come, too," Worthy said.

"No, you won't." Jessie shook her head. "You're going home with your sister, and both of you are going to stay inside the house. You've just heard how vicious Kelton is. We don't want you dead, too."

Worthy sighed deeply.

Bert Hutchinson sent a boy to the stage depot to inquire about coaches north and to buy passage for one. Worthy and Melissa agreed to pay for the passage and to send money to Rio Bonito every month. They gave Archie Weaver spending money and enough cash to pay for his food and lodging for two weeks at least.

The last stagecoach to leave the city that night departed at eleven. It would take Archie to Santa Rosa, where he could get someone to take him on to Rio Bonito, only a few miles northwest.

Ki expected no trouble, and there was none. There were five other passengers on the Concord coach, all miners or farmers. He said goodbye to Archie and saw him safely aboard. Ki breathed a sigh of relief when the stage pulled out.

Kelton would not find Archie Weaver now.

Chapter 19

"Where would Kelton keep an important paper such as the tontine?" Worthy asked the group.

"In the pond inside his house," Ki responded quickly. "Carlotta said he keeps all his really important papers there."

The four were sitting in the Bancroft library late at night. Ki had just come from seeing Archie Weaver off on the stage.

"But she told you that safe is impossible. Isn't that what you told us?" Melissa asked.

"Yes, that's what she said, all right," Ki replied.

"I've been thinking about it," Jessie said. "Maybe we can get into that house after all."

"How?"

Jessie smiled. "A diversion. We cause a ruckus on one side and slip into the house on the other."

Melissa asked, "Will that work?"

"It's worked before. Even the Bible mentions such a plan."

Ki scratched his chin thoughtfully. "You may be right. I'll go look the house over again tomorrow night."

Jessie nodded. "I'll come with you."

Jessie met Ki at the Nugget Hotel late the next evening. They waited till well after midnight before riding to the vicinity of Kelton's hillside mansion.

The house was dark. There were no lights inside that they

could see, but outside there were lanterns every four or five paces lighting the grounds. Ki had remembered correctly. There was no shrubbery around the house to conceal an intruder.

Jessie and Ki watched the guards stroll around the outside of the house in pairs. Jessie noted six of them.

She and Ki watched for over an hour, till they were familiar with the appearance of the guards. There were three pairs, and they strolled—talking and smoking—in no particular hurry. Theirs was an easy job.

Just as Jessie was about to speak, Ki pointed out the dormer windows on the roof. "I'll go in one of them and find my way down to the pond."

Jessie said, "I think I should go with you."

"No, not this time. Don't you think it would be better if you stayed outside to keep the diversion going?"

"Possibly, but you could get trapped in there."

He smiled. "I'll try not to be."

They moved away from the house and crept back to the horses. Ki asked, "What kind of diversion would be best?"

"What about fire? That's always good, like the Fourth of July."

"Excellent. Maybe Silas can get us some fireworks."

Silas Dent sent Jessie and Ki to a Chinese friend, Cheng Low, who had a warehouse full of fireworks left over from the last Chinese New Year. They were able to buy rockets, firecrackers, and a dozen other interesting forms of explosives.

Cheng knew little English. As he showed them around he would hold up a rocket or a firework, throw his arms into the air and yell: "Boom!" They enjoyed shopping and came away with a large basket filled with Booms.

Jessie thought it would be best to enter the house when Kelton was away. Ki visited Carlotta again to find out something about Kelton's schedule.

She was delighted to see him. "Where have you been!" She was more puzzled than demanding.

"I've been away," he lied, "on business."

She was somewhat mollified. "I missed you."

"Are you working at the saloon again?"

She nodded. "I have to live, you know. He pays me well. I'm singing with the troupe and dancing on the stage again."

"And what about Kelton?"

She made a sour face. "He's away somewhere on business himself. But let's not talk about him." She slid her arms about his neck.

Ki picked her up and carried her into the bedroom.

Jessie and Ki decided to hit the Kelton house the very next night. Kelton was away, but no telling how long he would stay away, wherever he was.

They divided the fireworks into two cloth sacks and rode to the same place they'd left the horses before. It was a still, overcast night. The fog hung over their heads, and Jessica prayed it would sink to the ground and give them cover. It might help to confuse their enemies.

They had also brought along a gallon of kerosene, which Jessie thought might come in handy. She pointed out that the fence surrounding the Kelton property would be a convenient place to fasten some of the rockets. They spent nearly an hour placing rockets every few feet and cutting the fuses so they would go off one after the other. They aimed the rockets at the house.

The two laid out large firecrackers in rows so they could easily be snatched up and lit from a punk. Jessie hoped the firecrackers would sound like gunshots.

When all was ready, Ki hurried around to the far side of the mansion and slid over the fence to lie in the grass, watching. Jessie had insisted that he carry a revolver with him. He had shoved it into his belt at the small of his back.

The first rocket went up with a loud *whoosh*!

The first was followed by two more, each hitting the house with a fiery splash! The guards shouted and ran, and a bell started ringing inside the house.

Jumping to his feet, Ki rushed toward the house. He spotted an ell where a trellis had been placed beside a window. There was no vine on it, but he thought it would support his weight. As he ran to the trellis, he heard firecrackers exploding on the far side of the house; Jessie was tossing them at the guards.

Swiftly, he climbed his improvised ladder, gaining the roof in a matter of moments. The dormer window was only a few yards away, staring at him invitingly. The window was unlocked; who would expect an intruder to get through the house's defenses?

Ki slipped inside and found himself in an unused bedroom, its bed and furniture covered with dust-laden sheets. He peeked into the hallway and saw a staircase directly in front of him.

Taking a deep breath, he crept noiselessly down the stairs. Exploding rockets made a devilish racket outside; the multicolored flashes brightened the dark interior walls, enabling him to see where he was going. As firecrackers exploded, two and three at a time, he thought he heard the guards replying with pistol fire.

Now on the main floor, Ki looked for the door to the basement. From Carlotta's description of the layout, he headed straight for the cellar door; it led down into pitch blackness. He turned and grabbed a candelabra from a hall table. Once inside the basement entrance, he lighted the candles and quickly descended the stairs into a dank, cavernous room. There before him was an expanse of black water, probably fifteen feet across, and no telling how deep.

Carlotta hadn't been specific enough about how to get to the safe on the bottom. He would have to figure that out by himself. He inched his way around the pool, holding the candelabra up for light, and found nothing. The coping was smooth.

But there had to be a way to bring up the safe!

He circled the pool again, this time feeling below the coping in the water, and found a metal ring. When he pulled the ring, a thin chain broke the surface of the water; the chain was attached to what looked to be a steel box.

Placing the dripping box on the floor, he examined the lock. It was a simple latch, which he opened easily. Inside was another box, quite dry. It was well locked.

Ki swore. He turned the steel box over and managed to get

the inner box out. It was not very heavy. He fastened the steel outer box and dumped it back into the pond, grabbed up the small box and the candelabra, and retraced his steps. He and Jessie would break open the box later.

The fireworks seemed to be dying out. Perhaps Jessie had used up most of them. Then too, the sounds seemed to be coming from a greater distance than before. The guards had probably approached her and driven her back. Had they discovered that only one woman faced them?

Ki took the basement stairs two at a time. There were lights on now in the first-floor rooms, and he could hear the murmur of voices. Some of the guards were probably wondering about the fireworks attack. To get to the upper stairs, he had to go past one lighted doorway.

Ki put the candelabra back where he found it, squeezed out all the tiny flames, glanced around the open doorway, and looked directly into the eyes of a guard!

The jig was up! Ki rushed across the doorway as the guard stood there with his mouth open, too astonished for the moment to yell. Ki gained the stairs and took them three at a time.

The guard must have come to his senses, because his yell brought men spilling into the hallway. All of them shouted at once, but they rushed into all the rooms on the main floor. It never occurred to anyone, apparently, that the intruder would go up. This bought Ki precious seconds.

He slipped into the unused bedroom and locked the door behind him. Silently, he climbed through the window to the roof and scuttled along it to the trellis. He could hear the men yelling inside the house.

Just as he reached the trellis, he heard the fire department approaching, bells clanging. The rockets must have set fire to the house!

Jumping to the ground, he ran across the sloping yard to the fence and slid over it, clutching the small box.

They had done it!

People gathered to watch the fire and the brilliant fireworks display, chattering, wondering what it all meant. Ki joined them and edged his way around to get a good look at the front of the house. The facade was still burning. Jessie had done an excellent job of arson.

He waited to see the firemen unroll hoses and pump water on the flames; then he strolled back to where he and Jessie had left their horses.

"Some show!" he said appreciatively.

Jessie grinned and patted the box as he fastened it behind the cantle. "I haven't had this much fun in years!"

He frowned. "I thought I heard shooting."

"Yes, they were shooting at me, all right; but they couldn't see me very well. They were in the light, and I was in the dark. Anyhow, when the shooting got too much, I splashed kerosene on the grass and touched it off. They ran like hares!"

Ki laughed. He told her how he'd found the steel box in the pond and pulled it out. "I hope there's something inside that we can use against Kelton."

Jessie held up her crossed fingers and nodded.

Chapter 20

When Jessie and Ki emptied Kelton's small strongbox in the safety of the Bancroft house, they found mortgage papers and various other deeds and documents, but no tontine.

"Is Kelton bluffing?" Worthy asked. "Maybe he's lost his copy of the tontine."

"Or has it someplace more secure," said Jessie. "Didn't Silas Dent say he controlled two banks?"

"That must be it!" Worthy snapped his fingers. "His really important papers are in some bank vault."

Melissa moaned. "Then there's no chance in the world. We could never get into a bank vault!"

Jessie examined the stack of papers they had taken from the box. "I'm not so sure." She held up a paper. "Here's a document detailing what purports to be facts about a man named Harold C. Coffin."

Melissa and Worthy both looked surprised.

Melissa said, "Why, he's the president of the San Francisco Merchants Bank!"

"Yes, that's what it says here." Jessie passed the paper around. "But it also says that he borrowed money from suspect sources to start the bank. Sources that would not stand the light of day."

Worthy passed it to Melissa, who handed it to Ki.

"It lists all the sources and amounts," Ki said. "Hmmm,

the implication is that this Harold Coffin is linked with crime figures."

"Is Kelton blackmailing Mr. Coffin then?" Melissa asked. "Is that how he controls the bank?"

Jessie nodded. "It could very well be." She smiled and glanced at Ki. "We should go calling on Mr. Coffin."

Worthy said, "You know, what we're doing will not stand up in any court of law."

Jessie looked at him sternly. "We're fighting fire with fire. Kelton is a cancer that must be cut out at the root." She looked from Worthy to Melissa. "Remember, he's already murdered your father and crippled your mother."

"That's right," Melissa said.

"Ki and I will go to the bank," Jessie said. "You two stay here and lock the door behind us."

Harold C. Coffin turned out to be a short, stout man in his midfifties. Long strands of black hair looped across his pate, and he sported a neatly clipped beard. Jessie and Ki were shown into his office. Jessie wore her provocative yellow blouse cut purposely low. Coffin's eyes went straight to her bosom, as Jessie had intended, and he caught a glimpse of interesting bare skin under a shimmering necklace.

Coffin's smiles were extravagant. "How can I help you, my friends?" He obviously expected them to ask for a loan.

Jessie came straight to the point. "We need something in one of your vaults." She fanned herself and lowered her long lashes demurely.

"Indeed?" Coffin said in surprise. "But why ask me? We have a clerk in charge of—"

Jessie interrupted, closing her fan for emphasis. "What we need is in Josiah Kelton's box."

"Well, really! Mr. Kelton's box!" Coffin's astonishment caused his face to redden. He rose from his padded leather chair. "What is this? Why are—"

"Please sit down, Mr. Coffin," Jessie said, her voice controlled, "and I will explain." She reached into her purse and brought forth several folded papers. "We know Kelton controls you and therefore this bank. We know—"

"Get out! Get out of my office! Get out of this bank!" Coffin sputtered. His voice rose to near-hysteria. "I will not listen to—"

"William J. Harrigan" Jessica said, reading from a page, "Luke Gerstel, Hoskins Grant." She rattled the papers. "Francis Kapczynski, Martin Fuller. Remember them? You borrowed money from them. I have the amounts here."

Coffin paled and sat down abruptly, staring at the papers in Jessie's hand. "Where did you get that?"

Jessie smiled. "These documents are most confidential, Mr. Coffin. May I call you Harold? There is only one set in the world. Is that not so?"

Coffin's eyes widened. "You . . . you were the ones who torched Kelton's house last night! So you robbed his home safe!"

"We admit nothing, Harold. But we *do* have the papers." Jessie rattled the paper again and glanced at Ki for confirmation.

Ki nodded, and Coffin's eyes darted speculatively to the door. There was an armed guard in the bank. Jessica spotted the look and slid the revolver from her purse, cocking it.

Coffin's eyes went round and his mouth gaped. "Are you robbing me?"

"Why, Harold, don't be silly. I told you what we want. We will take nothing from you personally, nor from your bank. Just open Kelton's box for us, that's all." She lifted her gun for emphasis. "And please act normally, Harold. We wouldn't want you to get hurt, now would we?"

"And if I do open the box?"

Jessica smiled winningly. "Then these documents will not go to the newspapers."

"How do I know that?"

Jessica smiled. "Because we say so."

Coffin stared at them both and settled back in his chair. "What you ask is impossible, I'm afraid."

"Then we will be forced to go from here to the *Bulletin* and the *Chronicle*," Jessie said resignedly. "Will you and your bank survive the scandal?"

"You don't understand. It is impossible, because it takes

two keys to open the box. The bank has one and Kelton has one. Bring me Kelton's key, and the box is yours." Coffin threw up his hands. "It's out of my control. Kelton has one of our very few ultramodern security boxes."

Jessie glanced at Ki, then slid the pistol back into her purse. They had obviously lost this round.

She tucked the papers away in her purse and stood, nodding to Coffin. Ki nodded, too, and followed Jessie from the office.

On the street, Ki said, "Damn!"

Jessie sighed. "We should have anticipated that."

"Well, I'll go see if Kelton's back in town yet. We may have to kidnap him to get that key. He probably wears it around his neck."

Jessie smiled. "Carlotta would know that."

"I'll ask her."

"All right, and I'll go back to the Bancroft house and tell them what we've learned."

Josiah Kelton returned to find his house partially burned and two of his guards limping. A band of desperate men, they told him, had attacked the house with fire and dynamite, doing their best to burn it down. They were lucky to be alive!

Kelton was enraged. "How did they get so close!"

"They fired rockets at us! We were so busy putting out the fires—"

He shouted, "Why didn't you send someone for the police!?"

"We didn't have nobody to send! It took all of us to keep the house from burning down without getting shot!"

"And you don't know who they were?"

"No, but a couple of 'em got into the house. But we chased 'em out! We would'a killed 'em, too, but—"

Kelton waved his man to silence and digested this information. At least one had gotten into his house? He hurried inside and examined the wall safe in his home office, but it was untouched. Of course, he had nothing in it but a few dollars, anyway. But were the intruders real burglars?

Would anyone know about his safe in the pond? Preposterous! How could they know? Not even Carlotta knew about it. He very nearly decided it wasn't worth investigating, but there was a tiny, lingering doubt.

Kelton went down to the basement, locking the door behind him, and pulled up the safe. It felt too light. He opened it. It was empty!

He sat on the coping, a chill feeling up his spine. Someone had been very clever, very damn clever indeed! The attack on the house had been a diversion, and those fools upstairs had never suspected a thing.

Of course, none of them knew about the safe in the pond.

Had it been Worthy Bancroft? *Very likely*, he thought. Worthy had proved to be an accomplished fighter, more so than he had anticipated. He had foiled several attacks by professionals. Yes, it was quite likely that young Bancroft had planned this attack and robbery. And anyone with enough money could buy the information about his pond if they were so determined. Kelton, better than anyone, knew that everyone has a price.

The pain of this was that he, Kelton, could not go to the police. Too many of those papers Worthy took were not for the eyes of others.

Worthy Bancroft had stolen very serious documents against him. Could he negotiate their return?

Kelton stomped up the stairs and into his office, which had not been fire damaged. Outside, carpenters tore out the gutted wood, preparing to rebuild. First his saloon and now his home! *But why?* He wondered as he lit a cigar and studied the opposite wall. *Why would young Bancroft steal my strongbox? What's he after?* He sneered. *The tontine, most likely.*

But, of course, his copy of the tontine was in the Merchants Bank vault. He smiled and puffed blue smoke. It was perfectly safe there. Harold Coffin would—

Kelton sat up. *Wait a minute! There's damaging material on Coffin himself!* His strongbox contained papers proving that Harold had borrowed money from crime figures to start his bank! If that got out . . .

Would Harold allow Bancroft into the vault to keep that information from the public? Of course! He would do it in a second! Harold Coffin had the backbone of a sliced tomato.

Kelton jumped up and yelled for his buggy to be brought.

Ki dropped by the Gold Dust Dancehall, next door to the saloon. It was still under construction, but in operation with a temporary canvas roof. He sent his name back and was admitted to the cubicle with the huge star on the door.

Carlotta was thrilled to see him and embraced him. "What are you doing here?"

"I came to ask you a question."

She stared at him coyly. "Oh?"

"No, not that question." He smiled and took her hand. "I need your help. Tell me one thing. Does Kelton wear a key around his neck? It would be a very important key, something he would have on his person at all times."

She laughed playfully. "Why, Ki, how would I know that?" She pulled him close and kissed him.

He slapped her rump. "Tell me, Lotty."

Carlotta clung to him, shaking her head. "No, he doesn't. I never saw him with a key."

Ki felt depressed. "That's the wrong answer. Are you positive?"

"Of course, I am. What's all this about a key? If he had such an important key, it'd be in his pond safe."

Ki shook his head.

Carlotta giggled. "Was that you who half-burned his house down? That's all people are talking about here."

Ki sighed deeply and went to the door.

She followed, sliding her arms around his neck. "It was you, wasn't it?"

"Don't ask." He kissed her and slipped out.

That night, having evaded the guards outside the Bancroft mansion, Ki related his discussion with Carlotta. "Kelton does not wear a key. Carlotta says she's never seen a very important key."

Worthy said, "He could still carry it without her ever seeing it. Couldn't he?"

"I suppose so."

Jessica said, "What if there is no key? What if Harold Coffin lied to us?"

Chapter 21

Josiah Kelton drove to the Merchants-Bank, whipping the horse mercilessly. Jumping from his buggy, he rushed inside and barged into Harold Coffin's private office, slamming the door behind him.

The bank president looked up, startled. "What the hell!"

"Did you let him into the vault!?" Kelton barely restrained himself from grabbing Coffin by the throat.

"No, no, no, of course not!"

Kelton took a long breath. "You know who I mean, Worthy Bancroft. You did not let him into—"

"Bancroft? Young Bancroft wasn't here."

Kelton paused, nonplussed. "Bancroft didn't come here demanding to get into my vault?"

"No. But a Chinaman and a blonde woman did." Coffin sat down again. "They had papers . . . uh . . . proving where I got the money to start."

"They had *my* papers! Those papers were stolen from my home safe!" Kelton frowned. "You're sure it wasn't Worthy Bancroft?"

"I told you. It was two people I never saw before. Do you know who they are?"

Kelton sat down heavily, staring at the floor. He nodded vacantly, trying to remember. This was all very disturbing. What in hell did a Chinaman and a blonde have to do with him? And where had he heard of them before? He had read something or had been told by someone about them. They were dangerous.

Then he remembered, Virginia City! The two nosing around after W.R. But they had been taken care of, hadn't they? Obviously not! They were up to no good, but why were they picking on him?

First, they were up in Virginia City, then they burned his home and robbed his safe, and now they try to gain access to his vault! Who were they? The only blonde he could think of was that girlfriend of Worthy's, and his men had assured him she was a fluffy little emptyhead.

Kelton looked up at Coffin. "Tell me about the blonde woman."

"She meant business. She did all the talking, and she pulled a gun from her purse!"

"And they wanted to get into my vault? Why didn't they?"

Coffin managed a smile. "Because I thought of something. Something I read in an eastern paper."

"What in hell are you babbling about?"

Coffin leaned forward. "I'm babbling about saving your hide! I told them there had to be two keys to open your vault. That we had one, and you had the other."

Kelton sat back with a huge sigh, staring at the little man across the desk. "I'll be damned!"

"They believed me and went away. It's logical, isn't it? The banks back East are doing it now."

Kelton smiled, nodding. "I owe you, Harold. You did exactly right. That was good thinking."

"What will I do if they come back?"

Kelton shrugged. "They won't. But if they do, let 'em look in the vault. Nothing will be there. I'll take it out now."

Kelton removed everything in his bank vault, putting the papers in a leather case supplied by Coffin, all except the tontine. This he folded and slipped into an inside coat pocket.

It might not be well to trust to safes and vaults for a time, he reflected. They had not proved to be impenetrable.

He drove back to the Gold Dust Saloon, parked the buggy

in front, and walked upstairs to his office. Opening the safe, he put the papers inside and sat back in his padded chair to light a cigar.

The fluffy little blonde girl who was staying with the Bancrofts, Worthy's girlfriend, could she be the one in Coffin's office? He had met her, and she seemed harmless. But what about that Chinaman and blonde? Was there a connection between them and Worthy Bancroft?

He didn't like any of it and took it out on his cigar, viciously grinding it out in his ashtray.

Grady showed up just as the cigar turned to shreds. He had news. "You seen the morning paper, boss?"

"No."

"Them O'Toole brothers."

"Well, what about 'em?"

"Their lawyer got 'em out on bail!"

Archie Weaver felt as if he had been beaten by a gang of toughs by the time the unsprung stagecoach reached Santa Rosa. He had bounced and jolted for hours, it seemed. Even though the road was not bad, it was full of holes and, in some places, was washboarded.

He climbed down and nearly collapsed in the dirt of the street. God, he needed a bed! The driver tossed down his old brown bag, and he looked around, leaning on a hitchrack. Across the street was a hotel. He smiled weakly and limped toward it.

The room he got was tiny and on the first floor. He fell across the bunk bed with his clothes on and was out immediately.

When he woke, it was daylight again. He sat up with a groan, stretched a little, and sighed, looking at the brown walls. Where was he? Oh, yes, Santa Rosa, on his way to Rio Bonito. He was running from Josiah Kelton.

He poured water into the basin from the white pitcher and splashed his face, then patted it with a threadbare towel. He spotted a mirror nailed to the wall and stared into it. He looked weary and needed a shave badly.

He suddenly remembered that he had money. Young

Worthy had given him a wad of bills to pay for the stage, the hotel, and for food. It was more money than he'd had in years, even more than W.R. had given him. Worthy and Melissa had been more generous by far than their father. He wondered if guilt played a part in their generosity.

With his surplus of cash, he could afford to go to a barbershop and get a shave. He snapped his fingers. Why not? Even if it cost him a whole dime.

After the shave, Weaver felt better. He went into the nearest restaurant and ordered breakfast, eggs and bacon, the way he liked them, with three cups of coffee and a little banter with the stout waitress.

Then he stood on the boardwalk and looked at the town. Santa Rosa was nice, but he ought to get going on to Rio Bonito. He walked down to the stage depot and looked at the schedule board. The next stage to Rio Bonito was not until Wednesday, tomorrow. Apparently, only one stage a week ran in that direction.

He strolled back to the hotel and paused; there was a saloon next door. He jingled coins in his pocket and smiled. He was a man of means now; he had a shave and a good breakfast. He entered the saloon and enjoyed the luxury of ordering a beer.

Jessie said, "Kelton will probably take the tontine out of the bank now that Coffin has probably told him we were there. What do you think he'll do with it?"

Nobody knew. They all shook their heads. All four of them were in the little sitting room, and Garfield had just left some sandwiches and coffee and had departed for the night.

Ki said, "My best suggestion is to ask Carlotta her opinion. Her idea will be as good as any of ours, probably better, since she knows him so well."

Worthy nodded. "Kelton has three safes and more vaults that we know of, but the tontine is just one piece of paper. It'd be easy to hide."

"That's what troubles me," Jessie said. "Ki, be sure to ask Carlotta tonight. You are going to see her tonight, aren't you?"

Ki nodded, and his smile nearly betrayed his emotions.

Melissa said, "I'm still worried about Archie Weaver. Is he safe?"

"I don't know how Kelton could find him, by now he's already in Santa Rosa."

Worthy added, "He's been warned to say nothing to anyone about this affair. I'm sure he won't. He was the one who warned us how dangerous Kelton is."

Melissa nodded. "I don't know why I'm worried."

Ki arrived at Carlotta's house very late that evening and waited for her to come home from work at the dancehall. The stableboy drove her buggy, and Ki met her at the door, smiling.

She said, "I never know when to expect you," and slipped into his arms.

"First, I have another question for you."

She turned, opened the door, and led him in. "That's not very flattering. I'd rather you came to see me, not ask me questions."

Ki assumed a philosophical pose. "Life is difficult," he said, "and full of questions. At the moment, I am doing what I must and not what I would rather. When may I ask my question?"

She sighed and shook her head. "I suppose it's about Josiah."

"Yes."

"I want nothing to do with him ever again. I still work for him, but it's strictly business. He never comes into the dancehall, not even to watch the shows, and I never go into the saloon. Now what's your question?"

"Where would Kelton keep something, something not very big, that is extremely precious to him?"

Carlotta sighed again. "Something not very big?"

"A sheet of paper."

"Ahhh, something legal, huh?"

"That's right."

"Could it be folded?"

"Yes."

"Probably in his coat pocket. He fancies himself as something of a fighter, you know. It might be difficult to get it from him. And he has guards."

Ki nodded thoughtfully. "You just may be right."

"Was that your question?" She shrugged off her cape and looked deep into his eyes.

"That was it."

"Well, now I have one for you."

"Which is?"

She moved very close, slipping her arms about his neck. Her lips barely brushed his ear as she asked, "Are you staying the night?"

His arms pulled her body tightly to his as he enjoyed her intense body heat. "Only if you ask me real nice."

Archie Weaver did not mean to draw a crowd. He had been quietly sipping his beer, luxuriating in the sheer financial ability to do so, when someone asked him about the Rush.

"Yep, I was there," Weaver admitted. "Went into the hills in late '49 and stayed till about '54."

"Did you make any strikes?" asked the young man next to him.

Weaver laughed. "Hell, made a couple dozen, had a handful of claims, two partners, and we took lotsa gold out'n them streams. Whooped it up in town, throwed money around like it were corn meal."

"What was it like in those gold towns?"

Weaver launched into his practiced tales. He told those stories over and over again, and he always enjoyed regaling appreciative audiences. He went on to his days in the silver lode, and had a circle of young faces crowding around, all eager to hear what he had to say. And they were buying him beers.

He was extremely careful, despite the beers, to keep any mention of W.R. or Kelton out of the tales, remembering what Worthy had told him. But no one could shake a finger at him for telling what he'd lived himself. He kept it all general, a schoolkid could look it up in a textbook now. Of course, that just wasn't the same as hearing it firsthand from someone who had actually been there and lived through it.

167

These friendly people could ask him questions, too. What did gold and silver look like when it came fresh out of the ground?

Weaver was too busy spinning his tales to notice the young man who hung on his every word, taking notes.

That same young man expanded his notes when he got home. In the morning, he hurried to his office at the local weekly and wrote out the story, a tale of the Gold Rush and Comstock Silver Strike by a man who had been there, Archibald Weaver.

The editor approved the story, saying, "Nice human-interest piece, Jerry."

By the time the weekly newspaper bearing the story came out, Weaver had left for Rio Bonito. He never saw it.

The *San Francisco Chronicle*, on the other hand, picked up the story and reprinted it word for word.

When Josiah Kelton read the story, he was astonished. Archie Weaver still alive!? But he had been burned to death in the fire that had destroyed his cabin and his entire family!

Hadn't he?

Kelton sent a wire to the Santa Rosa newspaper. Was the reporter absolutely sure about it being Archie Weaver? How old was the man who claimed to be Weaver? What did he look like?

The paper's response was quick, and the answer stunned him. It *was* Weaver!

Weaver was one of the three who signed that tontine. Kelton had believed him to be dead all these years. It was a dreadful shock to discover he was not.

Archie Weaver had to be eliminated!

Chapter 22

The Bancroft household saw the article about Archie O'Toole in the *Chronicle*. Melissa almost cried. Some unknown reporter had endangered poor Mr. Weaver's life by printing it. Worthy was all for taking the next stage north.

Jessie restrained him, saying, "Let Ki and me handle this. It's what we do best, remember?" She changed into shirt and jeans, strapped a revolver about her hips, and saddled a horse.

Worthy stood by feeling helpless. As he watched her ride off, he thought, *What a tigress!* It was quite comforting to think she was on their side.

Jessie met Ki just as he was heading out of the Nugget Hotel on his way to fetch her; he had also read the article. The two left for Santa Rosa on horseback, taking the stage road.

Kelton called Grady in and showed him the newspaper article. "Archie Weaver is in Santa Rosa. It's just a two-bit town, so you should have no trouble finding him."

"Who's this Weaver guy, and why do I want him?"

"Don't ask questions! All you need to know is that he's got to disappear forever. Is that very clear?"

"Yeh, boss. How'll I know him?"

Kelton had written out Weaver's description and handed it over. "Ask at the hotels. Somebody'll point him out to you. He seems to be quite a celebrity there. He won't be expecting you, and doesn't know you. So you won't have any trouble."

Grady nodded and left the saloon. The next afternoon, he would take the stage to Santa Rosa.

After Grady left his office, Kelton selected a cigar and frowned through the window, thinking about the O'Toole boys. They were out of jail. What were they likely to do next? Probably they'd come after him in one way or another.

He had wanted to send Grady to take care of the O'Toole problem; but when it came down to it, Archie Weaver was a more important item than the stupid O'Tooles. Archie alive could cost him a fortune.

Kelton went down to the saloon to talk to Shandy, one of the bartenders. Shandy, a huge specimen with no neck and a very flat nose, had been a pugilist and kept up with that sport.

Yeah, he said in answer to Kelton's question, he knew several tough young guys who could handle both a gun and their fists.

"Send one to me," Kelton said. "I've got a job for him."

"He'll be here tomorrow, boss."

The next day, a lean, poorly dressed young man rapped on the office door and entered at Kelton's bellow.

Kelton was surprised and scowled. "Yeh? Whadda you want?"

"Shandy told me t'come up here."

"Ohhh, yeh. That's right. Come on in, kid. What's your name?"

"Tommy Bolt." He edged in and closed the door. His coat was old and stained and fitted too tight across the shoulders.

Kelton leaned back, studying him. "You know anything about fighting, Tommy?"

"I fought some bare-knuckled bouts."

"Did you win any?"

Tommy smiled briefly. "All of 'em."

"Can you handle a gun?"

"As good as most." His arm moved, and he suddenly had a revolver in his hand.

Kelton smiled. Reaching in the desk, he pulled out a cigar box and extracted several bills. "You want to work for me, Tommy?"

170

"Sure. Doin' what, Mr. Kelton?"

"Bodyguard. If they shoot at me, they hit you instead."

Tommy gave him the same brief smile. "All right."

Kelton handed him the money. "Here, go get yourself some better clothes. Then come back here."

Tommy put the gun and the money in his pocket and left.

Pierre Zarit owned a mud wagon that seated six and made the roundtrip to Rio Bonito and the Russian River once a week, usually on Wednesdays. Archie Weaver and his carpetbag climbed aboard with four others and made the trip, arriving after dark.

The river settlement had no hotel, so Weaver headed for one of the tiny burg's two boardinghouses. He took a room in Mrs. Jestle's, even though she snarled at him, saying, "No smoking in the room, hear?"

After settling in, Weaver opened the window and smoked anyway. Worthy and Melissa had impressed on him the great danger he was in from Kelton, and he had no doubts about that.

But was he safe here in this little town that almost no one had ever heard of? Or had he left a pretty plain trail?

He had been the only man of his description in the stagecoach and later in the mud wagon. If someone asked questions, he would be easy to pick out, wouldn't he? Even though he'd gotten a store shave for the first time in maybe twenty years. And after all, Kelton didn't even know he was alive. Or did he?

Maybe he ought to slide out and find a place in the hills. He was accustomed to living in the woods, so it would be no great hardship. And it might just prolong his life a bit.

He knocked out the pipe and went to bed; he would buy vittles in the morning and take to the woods. He could come to town now and again to read the newspaper and see what was happening in the world. Maybe even send a wire to Melissa and Worthy.

In the morning, Weaver went to the livery and bought a black mule and a wooden pack tree, telling the owner he was going to wander about and pick at some rocks, "just for the hell of it."

He bought supplies at the general store, packed them on the mule under a tarpaulin, and was headed for the hills by midday.

He crossed a wide, shallow stream, climbed a ridge, and looked back at the little burg. If Josiah Kelton knew he was alive and wanted him dead, he might have a pile of trouble making it stick. Here in the hills, Archie Weaver was in his element. He filled his pipe and lighted it contentedly.

He slapped the mule's rump and limped on. Summer was almost here; he felt like a young man again.

Grady reached Santa Rosa and put up at a hotel, asking first about Archie Weaver. The desk clerk shook his head at Grady's description. He hadn't seen anyone like that, not for a month or more. No one had registered as Archie Weaver.

Grady found that no one had registered at any Santa Rosa hotel as Archibald Weaver. He must have changed his name.

He spotted three or four limping men, but none answered the description. One bartender thought he had served a man who might have been Weaver. This was not as easy as Kelton had said.

And as Grady wandered from place to place asking questions, he began to hear: "You're the second one t'ask about him."

"Who else is askin'?"

"A beautiful blonde woman and a tall Chinaman" was the answer.

Grady had a beer and digested this information. Who in hell were they? He finally decided to wire Kelton and ask.

Kelton's return telegram was worded carefully. The two in question were to be scratched off the list. Grady took that to mean they were enemies to also be eliminated.

He had another beer and thought about it, three against one. Well, really two against one, one being a woman. He hated to shoot a pretty woman, but if Kelton demanded it.

Grady's ace in the hole was that they didn't know him.

He could not imagine why they were asking about Weaver.

172

If they were friends, why didn't they know where he was? Or were they after him, too? If they were, he'd be smart to let them ventilate Weaver for him, then he could take credit with Kelton.

He could not locate Archie Weaver, and he finally began to suspect the man was no longer in Santa Rosa. There were other towns in the area; he could have gone anywhere.

Grady learned that the nearest town was Rio Bonito. Should he go there to look? It was only a few hours' ride by stage. He went to the stage yard and found that a mud wagon made the trip once a week. Pierre Zarit remembered carrying someone of Weaver's description the week before.

Grady checked out of the hotel on Wednesday and took the mud wagon to Rio Bonito. On arriving, he quickly discovered that a man of Weaver's description had bought a mule from the livery stable, saying he was going prospecting. The stable owner, however, did not know in which direction the old man had gone.

Neither did the general store owner. Yes, an old man with a limp had bought vittles and necessities there only a few days ago. But where he went, the owner just shrugged.

Grady asked in the saloons, "Where's the best prospecting from here?"

There were as many answers as there were saloons; he learned nothing.

This was annoying. How could he follow a man who left no trail? The only thing he could depend on was that Kelton would not understand. He might just as well go back to San Francisco. Archie Weaver had eluded him. But he would be smart to wait a few days or maybe a week. Then tell Kelton how hard he had worked to try to find Weaver.

Grady hung out in the saloons, killing time. Then one night, a wizened old man asked him for money, saying he was a prospector down on his luck. Grady bought the old man a beer and asked him his usual question about prospecting sites.

"Go east," the old man said. "Over that ridge to the east and down into one of them valleys where there's a stream. I git me a grubstake and that's where I'm a-headin'."

Grady thanked him. The next day, he got a horse from the livery and headed east.

Archie Weaver took his sweet time, moseying into one valley after another. He found a pretty little stream and made camp by it. He had no intention of panning for gold, but he investigated the stream just to be doing something. He found colors and nothing else.

But while moving upstream with a fishing pole, he stumbled onto an old, deserted cabin. It was not yet falling down, though the door was missing. He swamped the cabin out and moved his mule and possibles in time to enjoy a light rain from inside. The roof did not leak, and he was pleased with himself.

Jessie and Ki had no luck in turning up Weaver. No one could tell them where he'd gone. Santa Rosa was a busy little town, and few had time to think about or remember others.

But they quickly learned about Grady. He was one of Kelton's toughs, and he was asking about Archie Weaver. They soon spotted him and kept him in view. Apparently, he had no idea he was being followed and watched.

When he took the mud wagon stage to Rio Bonito, they followed on horseback, arriving before he did. They watched the stage come into town.

"The man's diligent," Ki said. "He just might lead us to Archie."

Jessica frowned. "Should we take that chance? Archie might get ambushed."

"The only other answer is to remove this guy permanently."

Jessie sighed. "If we have to."

Chapter 23

Patrick and Terrance O'Toole were men who hated well. They had failed to burn Kelton out, had been detected, and sent to jail.

Now they were out and itching to get even. They no longer wanted to destroy Kelton's business. They wanted him dead. Even though they knew that if Kelton died under suspicious circumstances, they would be very high on the list of suspects.

It was one thing to suspect, and another to convict.

Terrance acquired an expensive rifle from a gunmaker on Mason Street and took it outside The City to practice in secret. He was a good shot and with the rifle scope the gunmaker mounted, he became an excellent shot.

While Terrance practiced, Patrick studied Kelton's movements. The man came to the Gold Dust every morning between ten and eleven, seldom earlier. He was driven in a black carriage that let him off right in front of the door and then parked in the side lot.

Kelton was vulnerable for about five seconds each day. The time it took him to walk from the carriage to the door and disappear inside.

But there were very few places from which to shoot opposite the saloon door. The best one was probably a rooftop with a high parapet on which to rest the rifle barrel. But it was several hundred yards distant, and Terrance would have to aim particularly well.

At three in the morning, when no one was around, Terrance paced off the distance from the saloon door to the foot of the building they had selected. It would be a long shot, and they must pick a time when there was no wind.

Terrance set the scope for the distance, and the brothers prepared their getaway. The building housed a row of stores and backed up to an iron works; there was an alley between, where wagons made deliveries.

It was no trick for Terrance to climb to the roof, only a single story. Patrick would remain with the horses. They planned to be miles away before the police reached the spot.

Josiah Kelton was concerned that the O'Toole brothers were out on bail. He paid for information and learned of the many threats they had made against him.

It might be the better part of valor to take a vacation.

He thought it over for several days. He hated to leave his business affairs in the hands of managers, but this was a good time to do it. Things were moving smoothly, and in another month, the saloon and dancehall would be completed.

Where would he go?

Down the coast, a friend had a cottage on the ocean, a delightful place, comfortable, even luxurious, close to a town with a telegraph so he could keep in touch by wire. He was sure he would be able to borrow the cottage; the owner owed him favors.

But as Kelton was contemplating the move, the weather turned against him. A rain squall appeared from the northwest, and then a week of drizzly, foggy days interrupted by driving rains.

He changed his schedule around, appearing at the Gold Dust well after midday most times. Rain was not his favorite element.

The rain also caused him to call in several carpenters from the construction crew. He had them cut a door into the side of the building with steps down to the yard, so he could go directly to the side lot and get into the carriage with a minimum of discomfort.

The O'Toole brothers did not discover this new door for several days after the storm passed on south. Terrance had spent hours on the building roof with his rifle, and Kelton had not made an appearance.

Finally, he said to Patrick, "Has he discovered us?"

"If he had, he'd of sent men to get us long ago. No, he's probably just out of town."

When they finally discovered the new door, they were wild with anger! Kelton, the sonofabitch, had outfoxed them without even knowing their plans!

It was impossible to get at Kelton from the side lot. They would have to think of something else. What if they waylaid his carriage as he went home nights? They quickly noted that Kelton had two carriages, both rather ordinary, with no coat of arms or other markings. Both looked like dozens of other carriages, and the brothers would have to get very close to make sure their prey was indeed in the rig.

It would not do to murder some prominent citizen by mistake.

And if they got close enough to identify Kelton inside, the driver would have a very good look at them. Did they want to kill him, too. Their quarrel was with Kelton alone.

"Hey, we could wear masks," Terrance suggested.

"As soon as he saw a mask, Kelton would start shooting! He always carries at least one pistol."

Terrance nodded glumly. That was so. Killing Kelton was not as easy as it had sounded.

They studied Kelton's home, which was now nearing completion. Could they hit the man with a rifle shot as he got out of the carriage there?

They watched Kelton arrive home only one time and gave up that idea. The range was too far, and it was much too dark for accurate shooting.

They would have to think of something else.

• • •

Archie Weaver was enjoying himself. He had supplies in plenty and money in his pocket to buy more if he wished. He did not have to break his back in some icy stream panning enough dust to eke out a living.

What could be better?

He spent his days tramping around, sometimes investigating the stream because the sight of a nugget still excited him. Occasionally, he hunted a rabbit to change his menu. He saw plenty of deer but did not kill one because most of the meat would spoil. There was no one within many miles to give it to.

He saw the stranger on horseback on one of his idle hikes. The man was moseying down the slope of a grassy hill, peering this way and that, almost furtively. Weaver thought that very curious. Could this be a pilgrim running from the law?

The man halted by the stream and got down to let the horse drink. Weaver moved closer. The pilgrim had a warbag tied on behind the cantle, along with a blanket roll. He was evidently fixing to camp out.

The man was also heavily armed, with two Colt revolvers and a rifle in the saddle boot.

Ordinarily, Weaver would have welcomed the stranger, but something about this one gave him pause. He stayed hidden and watched the man.

Weaver thought this man had the look of a city feller, and it occurred to him that this well-armed stranger just might have been sent by Kelton to shorten his lifespan.

He followed the man upstream. The man moved slowly, stopping to look and listen. In time, he came to the old cabin. As soon as he spotted the cabin, the stranger backtracked a distance, dismounted, and tied the horse. Then he crawled forward with the rifle. Weaver watched with growing interest.

Waiting till the man was out of sight, Weaver untied the horse and walked the animal well into the woods before mounting and riding farther away. He tied the horse about a mile up-stream.

Weaver limped back toward the cabin, circling around to approach it from another direction. When he saw the roofline, he crept forward until he could see the doorway. He had not replaced the missing door. Sure enough. The stranger sat inside the shack with the rifle ready, waiting for him to appear.

The man waited till dark, and Weaver lay watching him. The man finally rose and peered outside. Weaver could hear him grumbling to himself. Apparently giving up, the man tramped back to where he'd left his horse. In the meantime, Weaver packed up all the supplies in the cabin into a sack and led the mule away.

Weaver then followed the stranger, who could not locate his horse. The man wandered, cursing, yelling now and then in rage. Finally, the man followed the stream back to the cabin.

But now the cabin was bare and the mule had disappeared.

Levering the rifle, the man began firing in fury into the woods at random. Weaver ducked behind a fold of ground and waited till the bullet tantrum abated.

He was sure the pilgrim would stay the night in the cabin. The man had no blanket roll or food. He would need what shelter he could find.

Returning to his mule, Weaver led the animal to a cozy draw, where he made a small fire and ate a warm supper. Then he slept for several hours, awakening well after midnight. Quietly, he returned to the cabin, approaching it from the rear. He stood by it to hear the heavy breathing and the small rattle of snores from within.

Carefully striking a match, he set the cabin afire in half a dozen places. The wood was tinder dry and flared up like magic. In moments, the entire end of the cabin was engulfed in flames.

Weaver moved back, keeping the doorway in sight. In several minutes, the pilgrim emerged, staggering out, to break into a run. In the light of the fire, he was hatless and without his rifle or pistols. The stranger ran as far as the stream, then turned to stare open-mouthed at the blazing cabin.

Weaver aimed carefully and sent a bullet into the tree next to the man's head. The stranger jumped, scuttling like a scared hare, running downstream.

Weaver followed, firing whenever the man's pace slackened. The pilgrim ran into brush and fell into gullies. By morning, he was torn, his clothes in shreds, and tired to death. Still Weaver harried him, firing close to him, showering him with bark and twigs. The man stumbled and fell. Bullets tore up the earth next to his head, and he staggered on, trying to put trees between him and his stalker. But he could not. He finally fell in exhaustion and could not get up. He just lay there.

Weaver went back for the horse and returned, riding it. The stranger was sound asleep, and the noise of Weaver's approach did not rouse him. He finally woke as pistol shots kicked dirt into his face. He looked up at Weaver on his horse.

Weaver said, "Who sent you? Kelton?"

The pilgrim made no reply but yelped as Weaver raised a pistol. "Yeh! Kelton!"

"Get up."

Weaver fired as the man was slow to comply.

He harried the man the rest of the day, sending him toward the town. Late in the afternoon, Weaver turned the horse and rode back to the burned cabin, reaching it just before dark. Nothing was left but a blackened heap.

Kelton should have known better than to send a city feller after him. He wondered if the man would go back to report to Kelton or simply disappear.

Weaver went on to where the mule was tethered and made supper, satisfied.

Jessie and Ki had followed Grady into the woods and had watched in amusement as Weaver ran rings around the tenderfoot. They had finally decided that Archie Weaver could take care of himself, at least in the woods. By dark, they were back in town.

The next morning, they were eating breakfast in Mrs. Jestle's boardinghouse when they heard a commotion out front. Grady had just staggered into the little town from the woods. Several people ran to help, and Jessie and Ki stayed on the fringes, watching.

Grady had had a terrible experience, he told anyone who would listen. A wild madman had pursued him, shooting at him, threatening to kill him. He had been very lucky to get out

180

with his life! He had lost everything he owned, his horse, guns, everything. He had even had a cabin burned down about his ears!

Jessie and Ki looked at each other and smiled. It served Grady right for going into the woods heavy-footed. They agreed that the main thing was that Archie was safe.

Jessie said, "Archie is safe just as long as he stays in the woods, and he's smart enough to do just that. Let's leave a letter for him at the general store and get on back to San Francisco."

"I was about to suggest the same thing."

Chapter 24

Josiah Kelton received no wire from Santa Rosa, no news from Grady.

He went to the window and studied the sky. The storm had passed. This would be a good time to go south, but it would take a day or two to go over everything with his managers.

He thought of Carlotta. She would make a good companion for his vacation, but she had told him in no uncertain terms that they were through. Too bad. He'd get another, one of the girls from the saloon would do just fine. Maybe the red-headed one, Kate. She was a bold-eyed little minx and might prove far more fun than Carlotta.

That night, with Tommy Bolt up on the box beside the driver, Kelton rode home in the carriage. He felt disgusted. That afternoon, one of his bartenders had brought him a copy of the Santa Rosa weekly paper in which there was another story. This time the paper described a curious tale. A man had been hounded out of the woods by another, stripped of his possessions, and frightened half to death. The victim, who had given his name to the sheriff as Grady, had taken the next stage east.

Damn! He should have warned Grady not to follow Archie into the hills!

Kelton sank back on the padded seat and sighed deeply. It was incredible that, despite all his efforts, Archie Weaver and the Bancrofts were still around to thwart him.

As they approached his home, he could see that the work-men were almost finished with their repairs. Kelton jumped from the carriage and walked around for several minutes, looking at what had been done. Then he went inside, had a nightcap, and went to bed for a fitful night's sleep.

Jessie and Ki returned to San Francisco. Jessie headed for the Bancroft mansion, and Ki went back to the Nugget Hotel. A great deal had happened in their absence, as they were soon to discover.

The police had made another raid on the house, searching in vain for Carlos Ortega. Inspector Jenkins had been even more grumpy than usual and had stalked off muttering to himself.

Councilman Bert Hutchinson had been to see the Bancrofts several times, Melissa said. Once, he had been accompanied by his son, Conrad, looking for Jessie.

Jessie laughed and shook her head.

Worthy had found W.R.'s copy of the tontine, and Bert Hutchinson had studied it and pronounced it a valid and legal document.

Worthy related, "It was signed at the time by all three princi-pals in good health and good faith. We can't prove otherwise."

Hutchinson had pointed out that Worthy and Melissa were their father's heirs, of course, along with Penelope; so all the participants of the tontine were, in effect, still alive. The ton-tine was only concerned with survivors.

After that was cleared up, Melissa told Jessie the most exciting news of all. She and Worthy were nearly bursting to tell.

"Carlotta's diary, we finally deciphered it!" Melissa cried. "It lists hundreds and hundreds of illegal transactions and more than a few felonies, as well as several accusations of murder!"

The three hugged one another and laughed heartily.

Worthy explained that Councilman Hutchinson, acting as the Bancroft attorney, had gone to the district attorney with the evidence, and Kelton had already been served papers to ap-pear. A hearing was scheduled.

Jessie was thrilled with the news and sent off a note to

Ki, asking him to come over immediately. Their charade was over. Kelton was about to be undone.

Carlos Ortega was delighted with the news, too, as was his wife, Juanita. By the time Kelton was dealt with, the police would no longer search for Carlos. His dignity and freedom were all but restored.

After receiving the news personally from the Bancrofts and Jessie, Ki went at once to bring Carlotta back to the Bancroft mansion for safety's sake. She had promised Hutchinson to testify at the hearing, and it was imperative that she be alive to do so.

She laughed when Melissa told her about their efforts to decipher her diary's code. "Why didn't you just come to me and ask me about its contents. Ki knows how I feel about Josiah! I would have read it for you and saved you all that time and trouble."

Worthy and Melissa looked at each other in embarrassment.

Carlotta continued, "Thank goodness you had the diary. I noticed it was missing, and I was terrified that Josiah might have it. He would kill me if he knew what's in it!"

Ki spoke up. "You're safe here, and I will protect you."

Carlotta was shown to a guest suite, and Ki stayed with her that night.

The next morning, a carriage took them all to the court building, where they met with Bert Hutchinson.

He looked very pleased and said, "We drew a fair judge. Judge Phineas Longstreet is an honest man, and Kelton has nothing on him. Come on in."

As they were about to enter the hearing room, several spectators gathered at the doorway, trying to bring their weapons in with them. The O'Tooles were among them.

The bailiff stopped them, demanding, "Leave your guns outside, Pat and Terry. We don't want no trouble."

The Bancrofts passed right by, escorted by Bert Hutchinson.

The hearing room was drab and rather small, with only about thirty spectator seats. Behind the bench stood the national flag and the bear flag of California. Several framed documents hung from the walls, and two long windows overlooked the other buildings.

Jessie, Ki, and Carlos took seats in the first row directly behind the witness table. Worthy and Melissa took their places next to Hutchinson at one of the two tables.

As Melissa and her brother sat down, they saw Kelton come in the opposite door and head toward the other table.

He stopped short on seeing her and Worthy and glared at them. His attorney pulled at his arm, but Kelton shrugged him off, saying something Melissa could not hear.

Hutchinson approached the bench to hand the judge some papers. He spoke with the judge for a few moments, his back turned to the room.

Kelton's attorney finally got his client to go with him to the other table. Kelton was about to sit, still glaring at the Bancrofts, his face deep red with anger.

Worthy rose at that point, smiled at Kelton, and said, "Good morning, Josiah."

This infuriated Kelton. He gasped and swore, and Melissa half-rose as Kelton suddenly took several steps toward them. He pulled a pistol from inside his coat, and she saw his thumb yank back the hammer as he cocked the gun.

It seemed to be pointing directly at her!

In the next instant, a gun fired at her side. Melissa saw Kelton stagger. Another shot was fired, and he was flung back across the table as his pistol skittered away to bump against the wall.

Instantly, Melissa felt a heated revolver pressed into her hand. Stunned, she heard Jessie whisper in her ear, "Take it! It was self-defense!"

Melissa stood, holding the revolver, and the room was suddenly aroused. Men shouted, the O'Tooles cheered, and the bailiff ran toward Kelton.

The judge pounded his gavel and shouted, "Order! Order! Take your seats there."

The bailiff kneeled and turned Kelton over. "He's dead, Your Honor."

The O'Tooles whooped, but a stern look from the bailiff quieted them.

Judge Longstreet took in a deep breath and let it out noisily. He stood up and looked around, taking off his spectacles and wiping them absently. He cleared his throat and said, "I very much regret this incident. For the record"—he glanced over at the court clerk—"I must state that I saw it all." He fixed the clerk pointedly with a stare before continuing, his voice ringing with emotion, "Mr. Kelton pulled a pistol and aimed it at Miss Bancroft, who shot him."

He cleared his throat again and sat down. "A clear case of self-defense." He rapped with the gavel. "I declare this hearing closed." Turning to the bailiff, he said, "Please have the body removed immediately."

Worthy wired Archie Weaver at once to tell him the news. In a week, Weaver answered to say that he had just come into town and was delighted with the events. He was thrilled to be free to return to the city.

Bert Hutchinson met repeatedly with Kelton's attorney, dividing up the estate that now largely belonged to Archie Weaver. Kelton's one decent act was to provide for Carlotta in his will. The dancehall was hers, free and clear. Ki was sure she would not miss him for long now that she had such responsibilities and so many admirers. He spent one last night with her to make his farewells.

Jessie made arrangements to have her feminine belongings shipped back to Texas. It might be a long time before she enjoyed them again.

Worthy and Melissa embraced Jessie and Ki. It would be difficult to take leave.

Worthy's pained silence told Jessie more than words.

Melissa spoke through her tears as she said, "None of this could have happened without you." She looked from Ki back to Jessie. "We owe you our lives."

The fog had lifted, and the sun shone brightly. After one last embrace, Jessica Starbuck climbed onto her horse and beckoned to Ki. As she rode off, Melissa's words and Worthy's silence echoed loudly in her ears.